Shane

Double Duplicity

Tarnished Remains

Deadly Aim

Murderous Secrets

Killer Descent

Killer Descent
A Shandra Higheagle Mystery

Paty Jager

Mandy,

Thank you for
Participating in the
Goodreads Giveaway

Paty

Windtree Press
Hillsboro, OR

KILLER DESCENT

Contact Information: info@windtreepress.com

Windtree Press
Hillsboro, Oregon
http://windtreepress.com

Cover Art by Christina Keerins

Published in the United States of America

ISBN 9781944973056

Dedication

There is an online group of writers and law enforcement professionals that was a big help in writing this book. Special thanks go out to Judy Melinek, M.D., Wesley Harris, Bob Mueller, and my son-in-law.

Chapter One

Shandra Higheagle scanned the attendees at her workshop and continued discussing the materials she found most useful when working with a raku fire. Several hands raised. She smiled anticipating the questions.

"Yes," –she read the name tag on the man's holey shirt— "Wallace, what is your question?"

"I understand you and Professor Landers—"

Shandra snapped awake and stared out the window of the airplane. No one had asked her any questions about Carl Landers, but he'd walked into her art show at the Downtown Gallery with some young blonde on his arm, and heaven help her, she'd become that cowering co-ed Landers had broken and manipulated for three years before she found the strength to break free.

The pressure and heat in the cabin nauseated her as much as the memories.

After the initial shock of seeing Carl, she'd ignored

him. Not a smart thing to do during an art show hosted by her alumni college, but she didn't want to cause a scene for that same reason. Only a few people at the event, past instructors and a couple of the long-standing art enthusiasts, knew she'd been one of Lander's arm candy.

The fasten seat belts light went on and the plane descended. Moments later the wheels bumped the tarmac and the plane landed. Shandra gathered her overnight bag from under the seat in front of her and slipped her arms into her coat sleeves without punching the older woman next to her.

The woman met her gaze and asked, "Coming home?"

"Yes." She still had a two-and-a-half hour ride to her place on Huckleberry Mountain, but she wouldn't have to drive. She smiled. Ryan would be waiting for her in the Coeur d'Alene Airport. It was Sunday. He always took Sunday off unless he had a case.

"Coming home is the best feeling." The woman patted her arm. "Especially if there's someone waiting."

"That's true." Shandra's heart sped, and she shoved aside the incident in New Mexico.

There were many people rushing to be reunited with family and loved ones. She didn't hurry. Having someone waiting for her at an airport was a new, thrilling experience. Walking through the security gates, her heart fluttered at the sight of Ryan. He stood off to the side, holding an armful of bright flowers. Her gaze traveled from his work boots, up his denim clad legs, to the shearling coat. She smiled. You could take the sheepherder away from the sheep, but you couldn't take the sheep away from the herder. They'd badgered back and forth several times about him being the son of a sheep rancher and her growing up on a cattle ranch.

She strode up to him and met his lips. This was coming home. His brown eyes twinkled as she stared into them.

"I'm glad the plane came in on time. There's talk of a storm headed our way." Ryan handed the flowers to her and took her bag.

She sniffed the contrasting scents of sweet and pungent. "These are beautiful. Thank you."

"You're welcome." He grasped her hand, leading her toward the outside doors. "I plan to buy you lunch in Warner, grab some paperwork, and take you home."

"Home." Shandra wanted to dive into her artwork and never leave the mountain again. "That sounds perfect."

Ryan held his pickup door open and she slid in.

"What happened in New Mexico?" He lingered beside her. "You usually come back from something like this bubbling over with excitement."

She stared into Ryan's chocolate brown eyes. Over the course of their relationship he'd managed to drag everything out of her that she'd never told another person. But her anger at herself for a being a victim was something she hadn't shared.

"It's that old saying—you can't go home. There were several people still working at the college or part of the art environment around Albuquerque that still see me as the freshmen freestyling more than they wanted."

His gaze drifted from her eyes over her face. "That's all it is?"

She hated being dishonest with Ryan, but she wasn't ready to show that much vulnerability to him

9

yet. They'd only been dating less than a year.

"Yes. That and I'm tired."

Ryan kissed her briefly and closed the door. Her comment would only put him off for a bit. He was too good at reading people and sniffing out lies, it was what made him such a good detective.

She watched several people hailing cabs and climbing into vans as Ryan stowed her bag in the tool box and climbed into the driver's seat.

"Tell me about the lecture and workshop?" Ryan pulled out of the airport following the signs toward Interstate 90.

Shandra didn't mind talking about those two events. They hadn't been sullied by Carl's appearance. Except in a dream.

They spent the hour to Warner catching up, talking about the lecture she gave on Friday night and the workshop on Saturday. Ryan confessed his work had been slow other than the usual thefts of items from cars at the ski resort parking lot.

Pulling into Warner, Ryan asked, "Deli or fancy?"

Shandra smiled. This was why she and Ryan got along. He didn't order her to do things or tell her where she would eat, he gave her equal say. "I'm feeling like deli. They wined and dined me more than I care for while I was in Albuquerque."

"That works for me. I'm hungry and didn't want to wait at a restaurant to be served." Ryan aimed a dimple-impacted smile her direction and she sighed.

Yes, she could still sigh like a young girl when Ryan flashed her with that smile.

He pulled up to a parking spot in front of the deli. She waited in the vehicle as Ryan trudged around the hood of the pickup and through the snow piled along the street. February in northern Idaho could be snowy and cold or balmy and sunny. Today snow mounds had to be scaled to get from the street to the shoveled sidewalks.

Ryan opened the passenger door and held out a hand. "Careful, those fancy boots of yours don't have much traction in this crusty snow."

Shandra stepped out of the pickup and wrapped an arm around Ryan's. "I should have left my winter boots in the truck when you brought me to the airport."

"But then I wouldn't have you clinging to my arm."

She looked up into his eyes. They stood on the sidewalk a moment, just studying one another.

"Greer, you gonna enter that door or keep others out?"

Shandra peered over her shoulder at the same time as Ryan.

"Sheriff Oldham, sorry to be blocking your way." Ryan drew her to the side and allowed a man in his late fifties-early sixties to step up to the deli door.

"This the reason you took the next two days off?" The sheriff stopped in front of them.

"Sheriff Oldham, this is Shandra Higheagle. Shandra, this is my boss, Sheriff Oldham." Ryan made the introductions.

Sheriff Oldham's eyes widened. "Higheagle? The woman from the art gallery homicide?"

"Yes, that's where we met. She wasn't and still isn't a suspect." Ryan squeezed her arm. "We caught the man who killed the gallery owner."

"That might be true, but she's been mentioned in

nearly every one of your reports in the Huckleberry area since then." The sheriff leveled his gaze on Shandra. "Why do you come up in all of Detective Greer's homicide reports?"

Shandra shrugged. "Many of the murders have happened in and around my property or to people I know."

Sheriff Oldham nodded. "Why is there so much murder around you?"

Her cheeks heated. "I don't know. Not luck, that's for sure."

The man laughed. "That's true. No one would call being in the middle of murder lucky." He grabbed the door and opened it, ushering them inside.

Shandra was pleased the sheriff ordered and took his food with him. She didn't like being under his scrutiny. Neither she nor Ryan ever mentioned to anyone that her dreams helped to solve many of the murders she'd been involved in lately.

Chapter Two

Ryan woke early Wednesday morning in the guest room at Shandra's house. He'd been staying in this room on and off the last few months, either when he had work in the Huckleberry area, or when he took time off. He was ready to move in permanently, but she wasn't. And he was willing to wait. Something in her past had spooked her from getting too close to a man. She wasn't comfortable enough yet to tell him, but he hoped with patience and persistence she would. Then he'd see if she was ready to commit to him.

He padded out to the kitchen to start a pot of coffee and noticed Shandra's parka missing from the hook by the back door. Was she out at the studio already?

He wandered back into the bedroom and dressed, planning to take a cup of coffee out to Shandra.

The buzzing of his cell phone stopped him in front of the window and he gazed out into the forest beyond the backyard. "Greer."

"We have a body on the ski slope." He recognized

the voice of Hazel Wells, the volunteer day dispatch for the town of Huckleberry.

"On my way." He scribbled a note and placed it on the kitchen counter. He didn't like running out like this, but he had a job to do.

**

Shandra walked out of the trees behind the studio and noted Ryan's pickup wasn't sitting in her drive.

"Where do you think he's gone before breakfast?" she asked Sheba, her pony-sized dog who stopped beside her.

Ryan had said he had to go back to work on Wednesday, but she'd figured he'd wait to leave until she'd fed him. Dreams had kept her awake most of the night. She'd finally donned her clothes, winter gear, and snowshoes at five and headed out into the woods to clear her mind. She'd never be able to work on a new project with the negative thoughts and emotions swirling inside of her.

The worst problem—she'd come to the conclusion the only way to let Carl's power over her go would be to confront the man. A trip to New Mexico again so soon didn't thrill her.

She took her snowshoes off at the back door and entered the warmth. Sheba trotted behind her leaving snowballs on the floor.

"Hey!" Shandra pointed to the laundry room and the small shower in the corner. "You know where you need to go."

The dog walked over and stood in the shower, waiting.

Shandra peeled off her gloves and coat and grabbed the showerhead hose. Using luke warm water, she melted the snowballs clinging to the long black hair on the dog's legs and belly then toweled Sheba dry the best she could.

"Go lay in front of the fire," Shandra told her big black mongrel. The dog gave her a slobbery lick and bounded down the hallway.

She laughed and entered the kitchen to make a cup of hot chocolate. A paper propped against the vase holding the flowers Ryan gave her at the airport caught her gaze.

Death on the ski run. Talk to you soon. Ryan

A chill snaked down her back. "What would someone be doing out skiing this early in the morning?" The lifts didn't even start running until nine.

***

At the bottom of the ski lift, Ryan pulled his pickup alongside a Huckleberry Police car and parked.

A large, Nordic-looking man stepped out of the ticket booth and strode forward. "I don't know how this happened."

Ryan stuck his hand out. "Detective Ryan Greer. And you are?"

"Daryl Svenson. I run the lift and groom the slopes. I found him this morning when I was headed up to groom the top runs." Mr. Svenson had a firm, hard grip. His hand tremored a bit.

It was clear finding the body had unnerved the man.

"Where is the body? Is there anyone with it right now?"

"I hauled Officer Blane up to see him before they called you. He's sitting up there. I came down to get you." Svenson started walking toward the large snow cat parked behind the lift building.

Ryan hitched his back pack on his shoulder better and followed the man.

"Any idea who the body is?" Ryan asked when they were both settled in the cat.

"Nope. Never seen him before." Svenson revved the machine, and they started crawling up the side of the mountain.

"I see the lift isn't even running. Do you think this is someone who went up on one of the last runs last night?" Ryan asked.

"I can't tell you. I don't man the lift." Svenson hollered over the loud purring of the snow cat.

Ryan stared up the mountain, scanning the open runs for Blane and a body. He'd first met Blane the same day he met Shandra. Blane was new to his job, a Barney Fife, who had slapped handcuffs on Shandra when he found her in the same building as the dead art gallery owner. Shandra was proven innocent, but you couldn't tell it by the way Blane treated her.

The fifth tower up the mountain, Svenson pointed the nose of the snow cat south, ducking under the lift wires as they rolled toward a small copse of trees. Ryan spotted Blane wearing a parka and jogging in place. Behind the officer, skis stuck out of the snow and a body sprawled on the ground at the base of a tree.

It appeared the unlucky soul lost control and hit the tree.

The snow cat stopped and Blane trudged over to the vehicle.

Ryan jumped out and strode over to the officer. "Any idea who we have here?"

"According to the wallet I found on him, Carl

Landers, Professor at a Southwestern College of Art."

Ryan's gut dropped to his toes. Was it coincidence Shandra just returned from that college acting secretive?

"Detective. They just radioed the coroner is here." Svenson stood on the cat tracks. "I'll go back down and get them."

Ryan waved the man off and walked over to the body. "Any sign of foul play?" Where had Shandra been early this morning? He hadn't believed her a murderer when he first met her, and he didn't now, but he didn't like the information that was stacking up so far.

"Don't believe so, but he's frozen solid." Blane nudged the body with his foot. Nothing moved.

Ryan pulled out his camera and started taking photos. He made his usual route of circling closer and closer, until the only object in the frame was the deceased's head and dark stocking cap. He pulled back out and took another photo of the coat's half-closed zipper.

"Did you unzip his coat to find the I.D.?" Ryan asked.

"Just this pocket in his jacket. That's where I found the wallet." Blane pointed to the right-side, outside pocket of the man's snow coat.

"Let's roll him." Ryan shoved the camera in his coat pocket and knelt next to the deceased. Blane took the spot next to him, and they rolled the stiff body over onto its back.

Ryan pulled the camera back out and started clicking. The man's jacket was open. If he'd been skiing at night, there was no way he'd have had his coat unzipped.

"Look around here for footprints other than ours." The way the man's skis stuck out of the snow, it was as if he'd stepped out of them and stuck them up as a way to guide someone to him.

"There's a set of prints… human and animal over here," Blane called from behind the tree.

Ryan followed the officer's steps and stopped. There were definitely prints of someone who stood behind the tree and that of a large dog or wolf. Ryan's chest squeezed with dread. The footprints were small enough to be a woman's.

The snow cat purred up the hill and stopped where it had dropped him off. Treat Maxwell, the son of the mortuary owner and part-time Search and Rescue member, jumped out. His teeth shone brilliant white in his dark face, like the snow on the mountain reflecting the morning sunlight.

"We got us a real stiff one?" Treat called out, packing the basket stretcher.

Dr. Porter, the local medical doctor and medical examiner, climbed out of the snow cat. He was the complete opposite of Treat. Dr. Porter was slender, average height, and so pale he was often referred to as an albino. Treat was six-five, broad as the snow cat, and dark as a cup of coffee.

Blane laughed at Treat. "More like a corpsicle."

Treat slapped Blane on the back, sending him head first into the snow. "Good one!"

"Men, this isn't the time to be joking around," Dr. Porter said, walking over to the deceased and gazing down. "He's dead." Dr. Porter pulled a paper from his bag, checked his watch for the time, dated the paper and signed it, before holding it out to Ryan. "Here's your official notice."

Dr. Porter turned and walked back to the snow cat.

Treat stared after the man. "I don't know which is colder. Doc Porter or this here man that's been on the mountain all night."

Ryan shook his head. "Load him up and take him to the forensic lab in Coeur d'Alene."

"This ain't a ski accident?" Treat unbuckled the body bag held down in the basket.

"It could be. But I won't know until a coroner at the state takes a look at him." Ryan took more photos as Treat and Blane put the body in the bag and carried it to the snow cat.

The four men rode down the mountain in silence. Ryan was good with that. Treat had a tendency to ask too many questions. Today he was unusually quiet.

At the bottom of the mountain, Ryan headed to the lodge. It was the most likely place to start asking questions about Professor Landers.

Chapter Three

Shandra tried to concentrate on throwing a new vase, but all morning she couldn't get Carl out of her mind. She'd spent years building up her self-esteem and working on her art to prove to herself she did matter and could live her life successfully.

"I'm giving him too much power," Shandra said, tearing down the clay she'd started to build on the wheel.

"Who?"

She jumped and stared at her employee, Lil. The woman had come with the property like a stray cat. But she'd proved her worth with the animals, keeping the studio and house clean, and watching over things when Shandra was away. Lil was eccentric, wearing only purple clothes that were usually several sizes too large, and walking around with Lewis, a large orange cat, draped around her neck.

"Why do you always sneak up on me like that?" Shandra asked.

"I didn't sneak. I opened the door and walked through just like anyone else." Using a walking stick, Lil walked over to the bench that housed the glazes. It took Shandra and Dr. Porter an hour to convince the older woman she needed to use a walking stick after her cast was removed. She'd agreed to use it for a month. Shandra knew as soon as the thirtieth day after her cast was removed, Lil would be tossing the walking stick to a corner of the barn.

Lil picked up jar coated with dried on glaze. "You had a glaze order come in. Thought I'd clean up some of the older jars."

Shandra nodded. The woman knew what to do and could keep things running smooth without needing direction. "That's a good idea." She worked the clay into a ball on the wheel and started forming the sides again.

"Radio said they found a body on the slopes," Lil said.

"Ryan left a note this morning. He caught the case." She dipped her hand into the warm water in a bucket by the wheel and slid her fingers up, building the clay into a thin layer.

"Some professor from New Mexico."

The clay crumpled as she took in the information. "Professor? New Mexico?" It couldn't be. What were the odds Carl Landers had come to her mountain and got himself killed?

"Did they say a name?" She turned the wheel off and spun on her chair, facing Lil's back.

"Don't remember. Said he was here on a vacation." Lil tossed an empty plastic jar into a bucket of water. "Heck of a way to end a vacation."

Shandra wiped her hands on the rag hanging out of her pocket. "I'm going to make a phone call." She grabbed her coat hanging on a hook by the door. Sheba was beside her as soon as her hand touched the door knob.

How do I ask Ryan who the dead man is, without letting on I know him? She entered the kitchen and started a kettle of water heating. A cup of tea would fortify her before she called anyone.

***

Ryan stood at the registration desk of the Huckleberry Lodge. He flashed his badge. "Did Carl Landers check in with anyone?"

"Yes. A young lady." The woman at the reception desk studied him. "Is something wrong?"

"Do you happen to know if that young woman is still in their room?" He hated telling people they'd lost a loved one. Working for the Chicago P.D., he'd offered to do paperwork to keep from facing the families of the deceased. He'd been assigned to that detail while waiting for his discharge papers from the Army. He'd vowed then to never have to tell another person they'd lost someone they loved.

"I haven't seen her exit the elevators this morning," the woman said. "Is there a problem?"

"What room was Carl Landers in?"

"Was? Oh dear, is he… I mean did…"

"What room, please?" The last thing he needed were tears and theatrics from the registration clerk.

"Room two-twenty-five."

"Thank you." He walked over to the elevators and pushed the up button. The doors whooshed open. He stepped in, thankful he had the elevator to himself.

The doors closed and the small car zipped upward.

On the second floor, Ryan noted the direction of room two-twenty-five and stopped in front of the door.

He knocked.

"Just a minute," a high, nasally voice announced.

The door opened, revealing a tall, blonde woman in her late twenties. Only a thin silk robe covered her curvy body.

"My, I don't remember ordering a cowboy, but I'll take you," she giggled.

Ryan held up his badge. "I'm Detective Greer."

"A detective. How nice to meet you. Come in. I'm Tabitha Vincent. My friends call me Tabby." She put a hand on his arm, drawing him into the room. "Why is a detective visiting me so early in the morning?" she asked, sitting on a chair and motioning with her bright red nails for Ryan to take the seat across from her.

He did to put himself down at eye level with the woman. "Are you staying here alone?"

Ms. Vincent leaned back and blinked her long lashes several times. "Alone? Why would you ask that? Are you the census police?"

"This room is listed under Professor Carl Landers' name." The muscles in the back of his neck tensed when he had a feeling he was being lied to. Why was the woman being so evasive?

"Oh! You mean am I staying here with Carl." She smiled. "Yes, I am. He needed a vacation, and I suggested we go skiing. Though why he picked this small out of the way place instead of Sun Valley I'll never understand."

"Coming here was Carl's idea?" Ryan jotted that information in his notepad.

"Yes. Why does that matter to the police? Did Carl tie one on last night, and you're here gathering incriminating evidence against him?"

"Does he tie one on often?" Ryan asked, adding that information to his notepad.

"He likes to have a good time. I had a headache last night and came up about ten. He was still sitting in the bar with Mr. Doring when I left." She narrowed her eyes. "Did those two get in a fight?"

"What would they be fighting over?" Ryan asked.

The woman practically preened. "Why me, of course. Mr. Doring couldn't keep his eyes off me. When Carl hit the john, Sidney asked me to dance. His hands told me, he would have taken me to bed if I'd let him."

Her smug smile and glittering eyes suggested Ms. Vincent was a woman who caused many fights.

"What happened when Carl came back?"

"Carl jerked me out of Sidney's arms. They glared at one another for a time. Then I told them there was plenty of me to go around." She winked. "If you get my drift."

Ryan shook his head. She was exactly the type Sydney Doring latched onto. Apparently, she was also Landers type.

"But they were friends when you left the bar?" Ryan asked.

"Seemed to be. They were talking about skiing."

"When?" Ryan had a feeling he'd be talking to Sidney Doring next.

"Well, today. It was too late last night to go skiing." Ms. Vincent stared at him as if he were the boy sitting in the corner with a cone-shaped hat on his head.

"It wasn't too late for Carl. We found his body on the slope this morning." He hadn't planned to be so blunt, but the woman had a way of taking over the conversation.

"What do you mean found his body?" Her hand came up to cover her mouth. Red fingernails stood out as stark red teeth in front of her pale lips.

"The man running the snow cat this morning found Carl Landers' body halfway down the mountain. He was dressed in ski clothing and his skis were stuck in the snow beside him."

"He didn't come to the room last night, but I figured he either found another bed or was picked up for drinking." Ms. Vincent's eyes glistened with unshed tears. "He was a lot of fun. Could be a bit demanding at times, but I like a domineering man in bed."

Ryan studied the woman. She wasn't overwrought about the news. Acted as if he was an acquaintance rather than the man she slept with.

"Do you know if he has any family I should contact?" Ryan poised his pen to write down names.

"He has a sister, but they don't stay in contact much. His mother, who is a piece of work, lives in Santa Fe." Ms. Vincent tapped a red nail against her cheek. "That's all that I know of."

A knock sounded on the door and shot Ms. Vincent to her feet. She crossed the room, tugging on the handle.

"Tabby, dear, I'm so sorry." Sidney Doring stepped into the room and pulled Ms. Vincent into his arms.

Ryan rolled his eyes and strode over to the door. Ms. Vincent clung to Doring, tears rolling down her cheeks.

"Didn't take you long to get here, Doring," Ryan said.

Doring's head snapped up. He glared at Ryan. "What are you doing here?"

"Telling Ms. Vincent about her lover. And you?" Ryan enjoyed the way the man flinched when he'd called Landers Ms. Vincent's lover.

"I just heard the news and thought I should see how Ms. Vincent was holding up." He kept the woman tucked tight against him.

"I'll be back later to ask you more questions." Ryan stepped round the two embracing bodies and walked toward the elevator.

In the lobby, he pulled out his phone to ask his sister, Cathleen, with the Weippe Sheriff's Department, to get the information about Landers' sister and mother. He hit the number for the department and spotted a copper-colored Jeep Wrangler pull into the lodge parking lot.

"What is Shandra doing here?"

"What? Who?" Cathleen's voice reminded him he'd dialed her for a reason.

"Nothing. I need you to get me phone contacts for a Professor Carl Landers' mother and sister. Mother lives in Sante Fe, not sure where the sister lives. The deceased worked for the Southwestern College of Art in Albuquerque."

Ryan watched Shandra's long legs carry her across the parking lot in confident strides. Her long, dark hair was loose, dancing in the wind behind her, as she headed toward the lodge entrance.

Chapter Four

Since she couldn't concentrate on her art, Shandra drove the forty-five miles to the lodge to see what she could learn. She hoped to bump into Ryan and invite him to lunch.

She stepped through the lodge door and met Ryan's gaze.

"What are you doing here?" He crossed his arms, stalwart as a tree.

"Since you said you had a body on the ski run, I thought I might catch you for lunch." Her heart raced and her smile wavered under his scrutiny.

"What do you know about Carl Landers?"

Shandra sucked in air and clasped at her throat. "It's him?"

Ryan stepped beside her, gliding an arm around her waist, and leading her to the bar area.

Inside the dimly lit room, he led her to a table in the corner.

She sunk into a chair and placed a hand on her

pounding temple. "It's Professor Carl Landers from Albuquerque?" She couldn't believe he'd followed her. All these years. Why did he pick now to chase her down?

"Yes. How do you know the deceased?" Ryan waved his hand. The bartender came over. "Two coffees, please."

The man went back to the bar and Shandra inhaled. She knew the day would come when she'd have to tell Ryan about Carl. She just wished it wasn't because the man was dead.

"Carl Landers was one of my professors at college."

The bartender set two cups of steaming coffee on the table. Ryan slipped him a bill. "We'll be good for a while."

The bartender nodded and left them alone.

Shandra wrapped her cold hands around the warm cup and stared into the coffee. "He was more than my instructor." She bit her bottom lip. The old insecure co-ed was gone, but she couldn't stop the emotions rolling through her mind.

Ryan touched the back of her hand. She grasped his strong fingers, willing his touch and strength to help her continue.

"I want you to understand, this was one of the worst times of my life." She finally found the courage to peer into his eyes. He studied her, but she didn't see the judgmental glint that she'd received from her mother and stepfather when they'd discovered her college lover was her professor.

"How was it the worst time?" he asked.

"You know Adam, my stepfather, couldn't stand

the sight of me. Which, we now know, was because of who my father was. But unfortunately, because of his lack of interest, when Professor Landers started taking me to dinner and saying all the things I'd craved as a child, I fell for it. And thought I'd fallen in love." She shook her head, but continued to hold his gaze. "It took me three years to discover he was using me and treating me like a possession, not allowing me to make friends my own age or allowing me to grow as an artist. Once I broke free of that relationship, I'd promised myself I would never be manipulated or allow a man to have any kind of hold over me."

He squeezed her hand. "That's why you've kept our relationship at a snail's pace."

"Yes. I don't want to get deep in a relationship with you and then discover I'm losing who I am and becoming what you are molding me into."

He raised her hand, kissing her knuckles. "I like you just the way you are. I wouldn't want to change a thing."

Tears burned the back of Shandra's eyes. "Thank you. I'm slowly seeing that. But you'll have to give me time."

"I will. But I don't have time on this case. Did you know Landers was here, in Huckleberry?"

"No. I hadn't seen him in years. Not until he made an appearance at my show on Saturday night. He smiled and held up a glass of champagne like he was toasting me, but we didn't speak. I didn't want to talk to him. I had nothing to say." Shandra took a sip of the coffee. "But that one encounter has been playing havoc with my thoughts and making it hard for me to work."

"Where were you this morning when I left?" Ryan

had his notepad out on the table.

"Do you think I killed Carl?" She drew her hand out of his.

"No. But you did know the deceased and I know you weren't in the house when I left." He shrugged. "Just writing down all the facts."

Shandra took another sip of coffee and studied Ryan. He'd believed in her when she was found with a dead body, he surely would believe she had nothing to do with a body found miles from her property. "I couldn't sleep. Like I said, thoughts of getting things settled with Carl were on my mind, so Sheba and I went for a walk. I think it was about five when we left the house. The sun wasn't even up but there was enough moonlight to wander through the forest. We came back, and I saw your pickup was gone. I read your note and went out to work in the studio."

"What time did you get back from your walk?" He took a sip of coffee, watching her over the brim.

"I don't know. I think about eight, maybe, eight-thirty. I didn't really look at the clock." She shoved the luke warm cup of coffee to the center of the table. "Any chance you can meet me at Ruthie's for lunch?"

"I still have to talk to Doring and I'm waiting—" Ryan's phone buzzed. He glanced at the phone. "This is the call." He slid his finger across the front and started writing in his notepad.

It was a relief to have Ryan know about her past, but his questions were uncomfortable. She didn't have a thing to do with Carl's death, however, their relationship was incriminating. They hadn't parted amicably. She'd had to get a restraining order against him.

"And dig up anything you can find on Carl Landers," Ryan said, staring at the names and phone numbers on his notepad. He could tell Shandra was still holding back about Landers.

"We missed you Sunday," Cathleen said.

"I told you, I had to pick up Shandra from the airport." Ryan dodged as many family dinners as he could. Not because his brother and his new wife, Ryan's ex-girlfriend, were there. No, since Chicago, he felt keeping his distance from family was the best. He never knew when someone would discover his true identity and come gunning for him. He'd taken down a drug cartel and shattered a gang when he was undercover. There were many people who wanted revenge on Shawn O'Grady.

"You could have brought her along. You know we all *adore* her." Cathleen emphasized "adore."

"She has that effect on people. I have to go. Thanks for the information." He hung up the phone, studying the woman sitting across the table from him. In over a year, he'd witnessed all facets of Shandra. But he could tell there was more about her past with the deceased than she was ready to tell. He hoped the information didn't make her his prime suspect, though technically, the death was still an accident until he heard different from forensics.

"Your sister?" Shandra asked, dropping her gaze to his phone.

"Yeah. Cathleen gave me the names and phone numbers of Landers' mother and sister."

Shandra cringed. "Don't be surprised if the mother sobs and the sister seems overly joyed."

"You know them?" Of course she did. She dated

the man for three years.

"Yes. Once I met them I understood why Carl behaved the way he did. The mother doted on him. But she was also very controlling. The sister hated him because the mother doted on him. She was sadistic toward Carl. When he tied me up the first time…" Her face darkened, and her hands fidgeted with her purse shoulder strap.

Ryan felt his chest constrict and anger burn a path up his neck and face. "He tied you up?"

Her eyes remained downcast. "Yes. First with scarves, then with rope. He said, his sister taught him how to tie a person up and not leave marks. She'd tied him up as children and would leave him for hours." Shandra pressed against her temples with her fingers. "I wished many times he would have left me alone."

Ryan's mind flashed to images of women they'd found in dingy hotels that men had tied up, used, and left for dead. "Why? Why did you put up with it for so long?"

Her head snapped up. "I'd been taught to do what an older male said, and he'd treat me so wonderful before I moved in with him. And afterward he'd tell me how good I'd been. How I made him proud." Tears trickled down her cheeks. "I didn't know any better. I went to that college as naïve as any teenager. And I craved the attention of a father figure. It took meeting another survivor of abuse, who saw the blankness in my eyes and who intervened for me to get the strength and the knowledge to fight back and get out of the relationship."

Ryan couldn't believe this cool, confident woman had been a victim of abuse. "Didn't your mother—"

"Do anything? At first she was appalled that I was dating my instructor. Then Carl smoothed talked her, and when I left him she was upset with me for walking out on such a nice man." Shandra stared him in the eyes. "I went to live with the woman who helped me break free. We became friends. She encouraged me to find a place of my own when my inheritance came through from my maternal grandmother. That's when I bought the ranch on Huckleberry Mountain." Her eyes lit up. "I love my house, my studio, the mountain. I was finally healing, finally beginning to feel good about myself."

She reached across the table. Ryan grasped her hand. He could tell she needed his forgiveness, though why, he didn't understand. She'd done nothing wrong.

"I found you and discovered not all men force you to do things that make you uncomfortable."

"Never." He squeezed her hand. "I need to make these phone calls and follow up on some leads."

"Was he murdered?" Shandra asked.

"I don't know. Right now it's accidental until I hear from the forensic lab. But I still need to discover why Landers was up on the run after ten last night and before eight this morning." He stood, raising Shandra as well by keeping hold of her hand. "I can't guarantee I'll meet you in an hour at Ruthie's, but I'll try."

She smiled. "I'll be there whenever you show. Thank you."

He stared into her eyes. "For what?"

"For not judging me." She kissed his cheek and walked out of the bar.

Watching her confident stride, he still couldn't fathom her being a victim. She'd turned her life around.

He could see where a nod from Landers would have put her life into a tail spin even after all these years.

He sat back down and dialed the number Cathleen gave him for Landers' mother.

Chapter Five

In her usual booth at Ruthie's Diner, Shandra sipped on a caramel shake but had waited to order any food until Ryan arrived.

"You all alone today or waiting for that hot detective of yours?" Ruthie asked, sliding into the seat across from her.

Smiling, Shandra replied, "Waiting for Ryan. He said he'd try to meet me for lunch."

The woman's grin faded. "Maxwell said he picked up a body from the ski run this morning. He's on his way back from Coeur d'Alene and dropping the body off at the state forensic lab."

Maxwell and Ruthie were engaged. She thought they made a wonderful couple and was proud to call them both friends.

"Did he say if it looked like an accident?" Shandra stirred her straw around in the shake.

Ruthie studied her. "Isn't that something Ryan would know?"

"He doesn't discuss cases with me." Shandra sipped her drink. At least cases where she was the suspect.

"Since when? You two have cracked every murder that's happened in Huckleberry since you found Paula Doring's body."

The door jingled when an older couple wandered in. Ruthie pulled the pencil from her curly black hair and stood. "He said it looked like the man ran into a tree. Probably broke his neck."

Shandra nodded and continued to drink her shake. What were the odds Carl would accidentally break his neck on her mountain?

The door jingled again. She glanced up and choked on the swallow of shake.

The blonde that had been hanging on Carl's arm at the gallery event walked in with her arm linked to Sidney Doring. During the investigation into the death of Sidney's wife, Shandra had a couple of altercations with Sidney and she'd charged him with assault.

Ruthie met the two and seated them on the side farthest from Shandra. She'd have to leave the woman a big tip for that one. But as much as she didn't want them to see her, she was interested in what they were saying. Having them clear across the establishment made it hard to eavesdrop.

Her gaze landed on the empty seats at the counter not far from where Doring and the woman sat. If I only had someone to sit on the end, I could sit on the other side of them.

As the thought sat in her mind, Maxwell walked in.

"Ruthie, you got something to fill up your man?" he called out and sat at the counter.

Shandra picked up her cup and wandered over to Maxwell. "Mind if I sit in that spot and you move one over?" she asked quietly, trying to signal him not to ask why.

He stared at her a moment, then shrugged and moved over.

Ruthie walked out of the kitchen as Shandra settled on the seat. She raised her eyebrows but placed a kiss on Maxwell's cheek. "How was the drive?"

"I was lucky to get behind a snow plow on the way back. Thought I was going to have to call a tow truck a couple times on the way over."

Shandra glanced at the clock on the diner wall. One. "You made good time for all of that."

Maxwell's white teeth gleamed as he smiled. "That's because I'm an expert driver."

Shandra turned her attention to the conversation in the booth beside Maxwell.

"What did you tell that detective?" Doring asked, his voice low.

"What do you mean?" the blonde whined in a twangy voice.

"Tabby, don't play coy with me. He wanted to know if I lured your boyfriend up the mountain. How did he even know I talked to Carl?"

"I told him how you and I had a nice dance and Carl interrupted. That you two had words, and I used a headache to go to my room. I left you and Carl in the bar." Tabby's voice took on a pouty, little girl tone as she added, "I was hoping you'd call me to come to your room."

"I thought about it, but Carl was so jealous, I didn't know what he'd do to you if he found out." Sidney's voice took on the husky tone of elk in rut that Shandra had witnessed when he'd tried to seduce her.

She would have gagged if the conversation weren't about a man who was found dead.

"He wouldn't have cared. I saw him eyeballing a young woman who came to the room with towels. We had an open relationship. He screwed who he wanted, and I screwed who I wanted. When we couldn't find anyone else, we'd do something kinky."

Shandra gagged on her shake and started coughing.

Maxwell's large hand slapped her on the back several times. "You gonna be alright?"

She couldn't talk for the burning sensation in her throat. The perverted man hadn't changed his ways, he'd just kept around a willing playmate.

The door jingled. Shandra dabbed a napkin at the corners of her eyes to catch the tears the coughing brought on. A hand cupped her elbow.

"I thought by now you would have headed home."

Ryan's soft voice jerked her back to the present.

"No. I said I'd wait."

He slid her off the stool and led her back to the booth she'd occupied before Maxwell arrived.

Ryan stared at Shandra after he'd seated her across from him. Her amber eyes peered back at him. "What have you been doing?"

Her cheeks darkened, and her gaze dropped to the half-finished shake in her hand. "I was eavesdropping," she said in a low voice.

"Why?"

She nodded toward the booth occupied by Doring and Ms. Vincent. "That blonde was the one who came to the gallery showing with Carl. She and Sidney looked kind of friendly when they came in. I sat at the counter to hear what they were talking about. Sidney is mad that she pointed a finger at him, and she's, well, she's just trying to sleep with Sidney."

He leaned back and studied Shandra. "Why did you feel compelled to eavesdrop?" He'd discovered all of that about the two earlier but didn't think Shandra needed to know everything. He'd learned from previous cases that giving Shandra too much information sent her into danger.

"Thought I might learn something." Shandra now studied him.

"About an accident?"

Her eyes widened. "That's what it's been ruled? An accident?"

Was that relief softening her features? He didn't want to believe she had anything to do with the man's death, but her interest worried him.

"No, not yet. I'm still waiting for a call."

Ruthie walked up to the booth. "What can I get you two?"

Ryan ordered his usual bacon cheeseburger, fries, and coffee.

"I'll have what he's having with sweet potato fries and no coffee," Shandra said.

"Be up in five." Ruthie walked past the counter where Treat sat. The man reached out with his large hand and smacked her on the butt.

Ryan grinned when Ruthie swatted the large man with a menu and kept on walking. Not only were they well-liked in town, they made for good entertainment when eating at the diner.

"What has you grinning?" Shandra asked.

"Ruthie and Treat. Those two get along so well. You'd think they'd get married. They spend as much time together as a married couple."

"We're starting to be as predictable," Shandra said, picking up a napkin and sliding it through her fingers.

He studied her face. What was she saying? "You asking me to marry you?"

Her gaze clashed with his. "No. I wouldn't…I mean…"

"You're not ready. But we do spend a lot of time together." He leaned forward. "Are there any more secrets about your past you haven't told me?"

Her gaze remained locked with his. "No. There is nothing worse than what I told you this morning. Carl was the lowest point in my life."

"And look at how you sloughed him off and became an independent, successful woman. Don't look back. You are strong, stay that way. It's the first thing I admired about you." Ryan meant every word. It was her strength of character that had pulled him in when he'd seen her sitting in the art gallery with handcuffs on.

"Thank you. I have come a long way and don't ever plan on going back to the naïve girl I was in college."

Ruthie returned with their food. "You two look like you're talkin' awful serious over here. It doesn't have to do with that man they found on the mountain does it?"

Ryan shook his head. "No. It has to do with our future."

Shandra stared at him, her lips tipped into a grin.

Ruthie slapped him on the back. "It's about time you two quit hiding your feelings."

"Detective Greer, are you following me?" Doring's voice boomed into the conversation.

Ryan pulled his gaze from Shandra and narrowed it on Doring. He'd love to find the man guilty of something. Doring had treated Shandra disrespectfully during his wife's murder investigation, and now he was flirting with the girlfriend of a deceased man. He never had liked the man.

"No, I'm not following you. Shandra and I had made plans to meet here for lunch before I spoke with you." They had decided to meet for lunch before he'd talked to the man a second time.

Ms. Vincent pointed a finger at Shandra. "Why you're Shandra Higheagle. Carl dragged me to your art exhibit over the weekend. Are you the reason he had to come here to ski?" If her loud voice hadn't caught the attention of everyone in the diner, her bright pink snow jacket would.

Shandra's face darkened and her eyes flashed.

Ryan slid out of the booth, putting his body between the two women. "I would think you would know that better than Shandra. She hasn't talked to the man, but you've been living with him."

Ms. Vincent narrowed her eyes. "You and her have something going on? That why you practically accused me of sending poor Carl to the mountain?"

He could see this woman was trouble. She'd spout anything that didn't throw light on her and her relationship with the deceased man.

"Shandra is a friend. I'm here having lunch with her as a friend. I'd advise you to move on along before I decide to investigate you and your relationship with the deceased further." He didn't like to threaten people, but he had a feeling if the woman didn't get out of here, Shandra may say something that could throw her under the bus when it came to suspects.

"My relationship? You might want to look at the woman behind you and her relationship with Carl." Ms. Vincent leaned around him. "I've seen the tapes," she hissed.

Ryan spun around in time to see Shandra melt onto the booth seat.

"I think it's best you get on outta here," Treat said, grabbing both Doring and Ms. Vincent by the arms and escorting them to the door.

Ryan slid into the booth and pulled a limp Shandra into his arms. What the hell was the woman talking about? Tapes? Shandra was white and her body slumped against him. He'd never seen her faint. She was strong. Or so he'd thought up until this morning.

Chapter Six

Shandra dragged her mind out of the black abyss. Someone patted her cheek. Voices murmured all around her. Her eyelids fluttered up. She focused on the face closest to her.

Ryan.

"What happened?" she asked, noting the feeling coming back into her limbs. She slowly sat on her own, pushing away from Ryan.

"You fainted." His gaze drifted over her face.

She glanced beyond him to Ruthie who nodded and Maxwell, standing behind her.

"I never faint." She ran a hand over her face and took the glass of water her friend offered. She sipped. "Why would I faint?"

"That blonde woman said something to you, and you melted like ice cream in hundred-degree weather," Ruthie said.

She searched her mind as she stared at Ryan. Why wasn't he saying anything?

43

His phone buzzed and he glanced at it. "I have to take this."

She nodded and sat up straighter, sipping the water. Blonde? What blonde? She reconstructed her day, and that's when she remembered. Tapes! What was the woman talking about? Unless Carl had taped his sexual encounters with her. Her blood turned to ice. With his death, those could come out. She didn't need this hitting the tabloids or news. And Ryan! What would he think of her? Her insides twisted with dread.

"You're looking better. Finish your food," Ruthie said, retreating and taking Maxwell with her.

Shandra glanced out the front window. Ryan was huddled in his coat talking on the phone. All she wanted right now was to slink back up the mountain to her house, sit in front of the fireplace, and hug Sheba.

Ryan entered the diner and slid into his side of the booth. "Are you feeling better?"

"Yes, and no. I remembered what that woman said." She reached across the table, hoping he'd take her hand.

He did and her heart slowed the rapid pace of panic.

"She said something about tapes. I swear to you, I don't know what she is talking about. If there were tapes made of…of…you know. I didn't know a thing about it." Her stomach clenched. "And I don't want to know about them. It will only bring back things I've shoved to the back of my mind to never remember."

Ryan squeezed her hand. "I believe everything you've told me. But I'm afraid there will be another policeman talking with you."

Fear pierced her chest. She stared into his eyes,

looking for solace. "Why?"

"You have a past with the deceased and recently saw him before his trip here."

She shook her head. "I didn't kill him. I didn't even know he was here until this morning."

"I believe you. But because of our involvement, I can't officially work on this case." Ryan didn't like that he'd been ordered off the case. Someone from the state police would take over the investigation because he was friendly with one of the suspects—Shandra Higheagle.

"Listen, I can't work on the case, but I can still get my hands on what they find out and see if we can figure out who really did this." He didn't like the way Shandra's gaze darted around the room as if she feared someone else would accuse her of something.

"Let's go to your place and go over what we do know." He tugged her hand, pulling her out of the booth and to her feet.

"Yes. I want to go home." Shandra slung her purse strap over her shoulder and headed to the door.

Ryan went to the cash register to pay for their lunches.

"She gonna be alright?" Ruthie asked, nodding toward Shandra.

"Yeah. There might be some rumors going around that she killed the man I found on the mountain. She didn't, but you know how rumors get spread." He knew Ruthie would keep any rumors about Shandra nipped tight.

"Shandra knew the man?" she asked.

"A long time ago. Thanks for lunch." He hurried out of the diner in time to see the back end of Shandra's Jeep moving down the street.

He was glad they had separate vehicles. There was a call he needed to make and he didn't want her to know about it.

Ryan slid behind the wheel of his pickup and dialed Cathleen.

"I heard you've been pulled from the homicide. Do the facts really point to Shandra?" Cathleen asked.

"Only if you don't take into consideration the type of man Landers was. They pulled me from getting any of that information. Could you pass along the forensic report when it comes through?" He knew he was asking a big favor from his sister.

"I'll email you a copy. You have to clear her. I can't see her murdering anyone."

"Thanks, sis. I'll be at Shandra's until we figure this out." Ryan hung up the phone. He'd caught up to the Jeep and followed her down the county road toward her ranch.

This investigation had brought out a vulnerable side to the woman he'd not seen before. She'd been wary of connecting with her Nez Perce family, but she'd discovered her father's killer and found more family, because she was fearless. Except when it came to Carl Landers.

The Jeep turned up Shandra's drive. Ryan followed, bouncing along the snow-packed road. He understood how living on the mountain gave Shandra the clay she used for her art and gave her a sense of feeling one with nature. But she was a good forty-five minutes from town and her closest neighbor was several miles away. Where Shandra liked the seclusion and believed she and Crazy Lil were two self-sufficient and independent women, Ryan saw them as two vulnerable women isolated from help.

Shandra drove her Jeep to the barn. He pulled up behind her and helped open the barn doors. She drove the Jeep in and parked.

Together they closed the doors, and Ryan grabbed his backpack out of his vehicle.

"I can't believe this nightmare is happening," Shandra said. "This morning while I was working with clay, I'd decided I needed to go back to New Mexico and confront Carl. To get things off my mind and get back my self-assurance." She stopped at the kitchen door and turned to him. "Now, I can't resolve anything."

He reached around her, opening the door. "Get inside where it's warm." He ushered her in and hung his coat on a hook by the back door.

Shandra did the same. Sheba lumbered down the hall toward them.

"Hi, girl. What have you been doing while I was gone?" She hugged the large dog around the neck.

"Go on in by the fireplace. I'll make you a cup of hot chocolate." Ryan shooed Sheba and Shandra back to the main room and entered the kitchen.

His phone buzzed.

"Greer."

"Cathleen tells me you're staying with Ms. Higheagle," Sheriff Oldham said without preamble.

"Yes. You took me off the case. I didn't think it would be a conflict of interest for me to continue to support her." He ran a hand over his face. Was his boss going to forbid him from even seeing her?

"I suggest you take administrative leave if you plan to spend your non-working hours with a suspect in a murder investigation."

"I think you're right. Take this call as me officially taking vacation." Ryan hit the off button and cursed under his breath. The only way he'd stay informed about the case would be through Cathleen and he couldn't jeopardize her job.

Shandra wandered back into the kitchen. "Was that information about the case?"

"No. It was Sheriff Oldham asking me to take a vacation."

She stopped at the counter. "Because of me?"

He'd never lied to her. He wasn't going to start now. "Yes. I'm too close to you to be objective."

"So you think I killed Carl?"

The sorrow in her golden eyes struck him in the chest like a cleaver.

"No! I don't think you killed him. I understand why Oldham thinks I shouldn't be on the case. We're too close and people won't think I could be objective." He poured hot milk in the cup he'd spooned chocolate into.

"Come on. Let's make a list of the things we do know." He led the way into the main room carrying two cups of hot chocolate. "Grab my backpack."

In the main room, he set the cups of chocolate on the coffee table and took his backpack from Shandra. Unzipping his bag, he pulled out his laptop.

"Cathleen was going to send me the forensic report. But since Landers was frozen, I don't expect to see anything until tomorrow." He opened his computer and sipped chocolate, waiting for it to boot up.

Shandra sat on the couch with her feet tucked under her. She held the cup of hot chocolate to her lips but didn't sip.

He put a hand on her leg. "Don't worry. We'll find the person who killed Landers and keep your past a secret."

"Can we really do that?" The hope in her eyes pulled at his protective instincts.

"We've solved murders before. I don't see why we can't figure this one out." He opened his email and clicked on the message from Cathleen. He opened the document attached to the email and started reading what had been discovered in the case so far.

Chapter Seven

Shandra sipped her hot chocolate and watched Ryan. Whatever he was reading had his brow wrinkling and his lips turned down in a scowl. She wanted to ask what had him so upset but also didn't want to seem too interested. Ryan said he believed she didn't kill Carl. His belief in her meant more to her than her pocket of clay on the mountain.

On the drive home she'd tried and tried to remember if Carl had ever mentioned tapes. Even when she had the restraining order against him and he'd called her every hurtful name, he'd never once hinted at tapes. Could the woman have just flung that out there hoping to get a rise out of me?

Ryan cleared his throat, took a drink, and captured her gaze.

"Why are you certain they will come question me? Is there something you're not telling me?" she asked.

"When I first arrived at the scene, I took photos and had Blane look around for tracks. He found a set of boot tracks with a large dog's print next to them."

She glanced to Sheba stretched out on her side in front of the fireplace. "There are other large dogs in the area. Or a wolf could have walked by after the person stood there waiting."

Ryan nodded. "But you know Blane. Who do you think he's going to say they belong to?"

"Me." She picked at the seam on her jeans. "And he'll say you are biased because you like me."

"I'm pretty sure the first call Blane made after getting to the Huckleberry Police Station was to Oldham to tell him I was unfit to work this case." He set his cup down and captured her free hand. "Don't worry. I know you didn't do it. We'll find clues that prove it."

"When do you think the state police will come?" She hadn't slept well the night before and didn't feel up to dealing with questions meant to catch her up in lies.

"Not until they have concrete evidence it was a homicide and you were involved. So far all they have is boot prints and large dog prints in the snow and a body. We aren't going to know what killed Landers until they do an autopsy. They can't do that until he thaws out."

"What about my past? I'm sure they'll dig up the fact I had a restraining order against Carl."

Ryan studied her. "When was that?"

"When I left him. He followed me around, threatening me, saying he'd ruin my reputation and I'd never make it as a potter if I didn't stay with him." She squeezed Ryan's hand with both of hers. "I went to the police, told them I no longer wanted a relationship with Carl, but that he wouldn't leave me alone and was threatening me. They sent me to a women's shelter that had an attorney on call who specialized in abuse cases. She helped me get the restraining order after Carl broke into my apartment."

"Did he ever once threaten you with exposing videos?"

Shandra shuddered and shook her head. "No. Today was the first I'd ever heard of such a thing. Do you really think he videoed…you know? I never gave a thought to that. Honestly, all I ever cared about was him leaving me alone afterwards." Shame heated her chest. How she had thought his exploits meant he loved her, she'd never understand.

Ryan pulled her into his arms. "You were young and impressionable. We all have something in our past we wish we'd never done. Wished we'd been wiser at the time." He kissed her temple. "Right now we have to focus on the present. How to find the real murderer."

She lay her head on his shoulder. It was good to know he believed in her and would help her find the real killer.

"Bring me a piece of paper and a pen. Let's make a timeline from the time you came home. Let's make sure there aren't any time frames that are unaccounted for. That way when the state police arrive they can't slip you up." He released her.

"I like the way you think." She crossed the room and picked up a notepad and pen from her roll-top desk.

"I picked you up at eleven at the Coeur d'Alene airport." He jotted the time and place down.

They continued marking days and times down filling in their time together and the few hours when she and Sheba had walked through the forest early this morning. It was hard to believe that was today. It felt like a week or better ago.

"So other than when I was sleeping and your walk in the woods, I can vouch for where you've been since Landers arrived at the lodge." Ryan set the pad on the table in front of the couch.

"When did he arrive? He had to be not that far behind me. Why did he pick Huckleberry to ski at? There are so many other places closer to him that have more amenities." She spit out the questions that she'd been thinking all day.

"He arrived on Tuesday, according to the registration desk. And according to Ms. Vincent, the blonde who was with Doring and Landers' arm candy, she tried to get him to go to Sun Valley but he insisted on here." Ryan slid the pen next to the notepad. "His coming here after seeing you in New Mexico isn't in your favor."

She nodded. "But why come here? Why didn't he talk to me in New Mexico if he had something he wanted to say?" She shivered. "I wouldn't have talked to him even if he'd tried. The minute I saw him, I felt like that frightened co-ed he'd sweet-talked and then conned into staying with him."

Ryan picked up the cups and stood. Rehashing her past wasn't going to find the killer. It was Landers' life they needed to discover. "Let's make dinner and forget about this for a while."

"I can try, but it's not every day the past comes back and smacks one upside the head." She followed him into the kitchen.

They had potatoes baking and a meat loaf in the oven when the back door burst open.

"Shandra! Shandra!" Lil burst into the kitchen, her

walking stick made a staccato cadence as she across the floor. Her purple knit cap sat sideways on her head. Her purple scarf hung loose around her neck and the three-sizes-too-big coat she had on swallowed her down to her knees.

"Lil, what's wrong?" Shandra asked, dropping the head of lettuce she'd been chopping.

"I was at the feed store picking up our usual monthly rations, and I heard someone saying you killed the man on the ski run." Lil stopped in front of Shandra. "You never left the ranch until this morning after they say he was killed."

Ryan stepped between the two. "Who was saying this?"

"I ain't tellin' you." Lil narrowed her eyes. "You'll lock her up just to keep yourself in a job."

"Ryan is on vacation. His boss didn't think he could be objective when it came to me," Shandra said, rubbing a hand up and down his arm.

His heart sped up, knowing Shandra stuck up for him. He and Lil were still on shaky ground around one another after he'd accused her of killing her fiancé thirty years ago. They both had Shandra's best interests at heart, but sometimes their way of dealing with it clashed.

"I won't be hauling Shandra into jail. What did you hear and from whom? It might help us figure out who really killed the man." He grabbed the excess sleeve material on Lil's coat and sat her on a stool.

"Did you go anywhere besides the feed store?" he asked the woman as she pulled the knitted hat from her head, causing a riot of spiked white hair.

"After hearing what I did at the feed store, I

moseyed over to the Quik Mart, you know cuz it's on the same side of town as the ski lodge and all."

"What did you hear there?" he asked as Shandra went back to cutting lettuce.

"That the man was a professor from the college where Shandra went to school, and that he'd come here to see her." Lil nodded her head.

The chopping stopped. Ryan looked across the counter to Shandra.

"He was a professor at my college, but as far as coming here to see me…he didn't." Shandra shook her head. "The last time I saw him was Saturday night in New Mexico." She stabbed the knife into the half a head of lettuce. "Why would someone say he came here to see me? Who would even know that?"

"Ms. Vincent," Ryan said at the same time Shandra said, "Tabby."

"What does that woman have against me? I've never even met her?" Shandra asked.

"Did you say anything to anyone?" he asked Lil.

"I told Harry at the feed store that Shandra didn't do it because she's been right here the whole time. I kept my mouth shut at the Quik Mart." Lil made the action of zipping her mouth closed.

Ryan shoved the information to the back of his mind. He could tell this was starting to wear on Shandra. She'd stood up to the scrutiny when people believed she killed the gallery owner but for some reason this death being pinned on her had taken her back to the timid co-ed she'd been.

"Lil, want to stay for dinner? We have plenty," he said, to change the conversation and atmosphere. There wasn't anything more they could do tonight. At least that Shandra could do. He was going to call in some favors with police buddies in New Mexico.

Chapter Eight

Shandra went to bed early. She was exhausted and couldn't make small talk anymore. Ryan had tried hard to take her mind off of Carl and the possibility that everyone thought she'd killed him. But it remained in her mind through dinner and their card game afterwards. As soon as Lil excused herself to her quarters in the barn, Shandra headed to bed.

Even though she was exhausted, sleep didn't come easily. Finally, hugging Sheba and concentrating on floating clouds, she drifted to sleep.

Ella, her deceased Nez Perce grandmother, beckoned her. Shandra shook her head. She was bound to a tree with vines. Ella motioned to break the vines. Shandra shook her head. Fear burst out on her forehead in droplets of sweat.

Ella nodded and made the motion of breaking again. Shandra wanted to follow Ella, wanted to be strong like her grandmother. She clenched her fists and raised her arms, breaking the vines that held her.

Elation and freedom thrummed in her heart.

*She looked up, and Ella smiled down on her.
Footsteps spun Shandra around. Carl was walking
toward her, smiling smugly, and carrying a small pistol
in his hand. Shandra slammed her back against the
tree. Ella grasped her by the hand and pulled her along
into the clouds with her. Freedom once again lifted her
heart. She was free of Carl, but not completely until she
found his killer.*

***

Shandra was up early the following morning fixing
breakfast when Ryan wandered into the kitchen.

"Good morning," she said, handing him a cup of
coffee.

"Morning." He kissed her cheek and sat at the
counter.

Placing pancakes on a plate and sliding an egg
alongside of them, she asked, "Didn't you sleep well?"

"I sent off some enquiries last night to some friends
in law enforcement in New Mexico. I wanted all the
information I could get on Landers. There has to be
more women than you who were charmed and then
disenchanted by the man." Ryan sipped his coffee as
she placed the plate in front of him.

"There were two before me. I don't know how
many after me. That was nine years ago." She sat
beside him and poked the egg on her plate with a fork.

"Did all of them last as long as your relationship
with him?" He didn't look at her.

This morning, after the dream of Ella setting her
free, she wasn't going to become that scared co-ed
again. She'd proved her strength the last eight years and
wasn't going to allow the past to make her a victim.

"Mine was the longest because my family didn't step in. From what I gathered from things Carl said about his previous conquests, a father or brother came and took the woman away."

Ryan captured her hand closest to him. "I'm sorry no one came for you. But it's a testament to your strength that you got out on your own."

She smiled and confidence bubbled in her chest. "Yes, it is."

He studied her. "You are back to the Shandra I met that day in the gallery. What brought about the change?"

"Grandmother came to me in my dream last night. She showed me I'd broken free and how wonderful that freedom is." She frowned. "Carl was in the dream. He had a small pistol in his hand. It was tiny, the size of his palm."

"I'll text Cathleen and see if they're treating this as a homicide yet." Ryan pulled his phone out of the case hanging on his belt and concentrated on the buttons.

Shandra ate her pancake and thought about the other women Carl had used. She hoped they all came out of the ordeal stronger and more confident. And that they each found a good man to have in their lives. Her gaze swept over Ryan. He was a keeper. But she wasn't ready to commit to anything with anyone just yet.

"Cathleen says this is now a homicide. She just sent me the forensic autopsy." Ryan went in the other room and came back with his laptop. "It's easier to read documents on here than my phone," he said, placing his laptop on the counter.

Keys clicked and his attention was riveted on the

computer screen.

Shandra wiggled on her stool, wondering what the report had to say.

Ryan finished reading and turned to her. "It was definitely a homicide. A twenty-two caliber bullet entered his skull, killing him instantly."

"Twenty-two? I didn't think a bullet that small could kill someone." She thought about the rifle she carried when on the mountain. It was a .38. Strong enough to deter any of the large animals on the mountain.

"Used the way this one was, it is deadly. It had to be someone Landers knew. According to the report, the bullet entered through his left temple. The stocking cap he wore must have been frozen over the hole. That's why we didn't see it." Ryan stared out the window. "He was laying on his right side. That's why we didn't see any blood. The forensic specialist says the barrel of the weapon was placed against the head and the trigger pulled. The smoke left a dark coloration and the gases from the firing ripped the skin around the wound."

Shandra shuddered. "How could someone stand next to him and pull the trigger?"

"It was someone who was cold and calculating." He read a little more then closed his computer. "Do you own a twenty-two?"

She stared at him. "No."

"Good. That's the first thing the state police will ask you when they question you." He sipped his coffee.

"Do you think the gun in Carl's hand in my dream is the murder weapon?" she asked.

Ryan turned to her. "The pistol that killed him must have been Landers'. Either he was carrying it and someone took it away from him…"

"Or someone staying with him took it from his possessions and planned to use his own pistol on him," she finished. Her thoughts went straight to Tabby, who was doing her best to pin the murder on Shandra.

"Finding that weapon is the clue to the killer," Ryan said.

"If it's small, it could be anywhere. The killer could have dropped it in a snow drift or tossed it in the garbage at the lodge." Shandra wasn't feeling confident they'd find the weapon.

Ryan dug into his food. "The good news is you don't own a twenty-two."

"Do you have people looking into Tabby as well as Carl?" Shandra picked up her cup. "She isn't Carl's usual type. He always picked the meek, but pretty, female students. Tabby doesn't strike me as meek."

"I am getting background on her. You're right. From what you've told me, she isn't Landers' typical arm candy." Ryan cleaned his plate and carried it over to the sink. He leaned with his backside against the counter and studied her over his coffee cup. "Any plans for today?"

Shandra didn't want to sound too jubilant, but she felt a new-found freedom since her dream and she wanted to express it in a vase. "I don't want this to sound callous but after the dream last night, I feel like I've been let free. I hope to reflect that in a vase idea that is floating in my head."

Ryan smiled and walked over to her. He put an arm around her and hugged. "I think that is a wonderful idea. I'll reach out to some more people I know in law enforcement, then I'd like to take you to town tonight for dinner. We'll go to the lodge."

She peered up at Ryan. "Do you think that's a good idea? I mean with all the rumors?"

"You haven't been taken into custody. I want to see how Doring and Ms. Vincent are carrying on. We can't discover that sitting here. We have to get out and mingle. Especially, since I can't work the case and ask questions."

Shandra smiled. She liked the way he thought. "In that case, I'd love to go to dinner with you at the lodge."

"It's a date." He kissed her briefly on the lips and wandered into the main room.

Shandra cleaned up the kitchen, called Sheba, and headed out to the studio. She hoped to get the main portion of the vase she envisioned sculpted today. She'd work on the cut-outs and details the rest of the week.

Chapter Nine

"You had a busy day learning all you did and making reservations," Shandra said, enjoying actually having a date with Ryan. They stood by a table in the Huckleberry Lodge dining room.

Ryan took her coat, placing it on the extra chair at their table, and held her chair.

"I promised you a night out." He took his seat across from her and smiled at the hostess. "We'll have a bottle of your best white wine, please."

The woman smiled and nodded.

"Are you going to get me drunk, Detective Greer?" Drinking sounded like a good way to forget her troubles, but she'd never allow herself to lose control, not even with Ryan to take care of her.

"No, but a bottle of wine is a good way to make lingering at the table look like we don't want to get caught driving drunk." He winked and she understood what he meant.

They'd stay in the restaurant until it closed, to get a

chance to watch Doring and Tabby together.

The hostess brought the wine and poured. "Your waiter will be here shortly," she said, before leaving them alone.

Shandra had a good view of the whole restaurant, but Ryan's back was to the entrance and most of the room.

"Let's get cozy," he said, moving his chair, place setting, and wine over close to her.

"I'd be flattered if I thought you actually wanted to sit close." She sipped her wine and stared at the door.

Ryan laughed and said, "I do want to be near you. But I also want to see what you see."

"Seven is a good time to come. I'm pretty sure Sidney wouldn't come any earlier than this to have dinner." She scanned the people at the other tables. Most looked like out-of-towners here for the skiing.

"We could ask if he plans to eat here tonight." Ryan sipped his wine while casually scanning the room.

Shandra picked up the menu and studied the specials. "We should at least look at the menus."

Ryan picked his menu up, spread it wide, and leaned over, kissing her cheek.

She turned to say something and he captured her lips.

The sound of someone clearing their throat, spun her out of the kiss.

"I see you two are busy. Would you like me to come back for your order?"

Cheeks heating, Shandra lowered her menu and stared at the name tag on the waiter's shirt. Tyler.

"I think we're ready to order." Ryan smiled at Shandra and nodded for her to go first.

"I'll have the salmon special, please," she said, handing the menu to the waiter.

"I'll have the prime rib special, baked potato, and salad." Ryan handed the menu to the waiter and asked, "Do you happened to know if Mr. Doring will be coming in tonight?"

The waiter tapped his notepad with a pen. "He comes in every night at eight. The last few days he's had a knock-out blonde with him. Are you friends of his?"

"No. Just curious. I know he owns the lodge. I figured if he eats here then the food should be good." Ryan picked up his wine glass.

"The food here is good." The waiter nodded and left.

"That was brash asking about Doring and kissing me behind the menus," Shandra said, picking up her wine glass.

Ryan's lips tipped up, showing his dimple and his eyes sparkled. "This is a date, and I believe kissing is allowed on dates. I didn't want to wonder and stare at the door all night when I have a much better view staring at you."

"Flattery may just get you somewhere." She teased. Ryan was easy for her to talk to and tease. He never took her remarks as more than joking around.

He added more wine to her glass and captured her free hand. "Then I guess I should keep up the flattery."

She enjoyed the attention Ryan gave her and the conversation. They discussed the paintings and art decorating the room while eating their salads. One of the vases she had crafted sat on a pedestal in a small alcove. Doring had purchased it at a summer art event two years ago. Which reminded her Ryan had purchased her vase at last year's event.

"Did Conor and Lissa like the vase you gave them for their wedding present?"

Ryan put his fork down and gazed into her eyes. "I gave them a blanket. I kept the vase for myself. I liked it too much to give it as a gift, even to family."

Her heart soared. Nothing else he'd ever said made her this happy. Not that he didn't give it to his brother and his new wife, but that he couldn't part with the vase.

"I see." She smiled and leaned toward him, kissing his cheek. "That's the nicest thing you could have said," she whispered.

He turned his face to her. "It's the truth. That vase captured something in me the second I saw it. The more I thought of giving it to Conor and Lissa, I couldn't do it."

She kissed his lips. "Thank you."

"What have we here?" a male voice boomed.

Shandra stared across the table at Sidney Doring, with Tabby clinging to his arm. The woman's bright red lips were tipped in a sneer.

"A lawman consorting with a murderer." Again, Sidney's voice was much louder than normal. He was drawing attention to them.

Ryan stood. "You could lower your voice. There is no consorting with a murderer here. We're simply two people enjoying a meal."

"Is this why the state police were asking me questions today instead of you?" The gloating tone, smirk, and flash in Sidney's eyes told Shandra he was probably telling the state police all kinds of lies. Sidney hadn't liked Ryan or her since his wife's death and their belief he'd killed her.

"I've been taken off the case. Not because Shandra is a suspect but because I'm not unbiased when it comes to you." Ryan sat back down.

"For a lawman, I'm surprised you'd want to be seen with someone like her." Tabby pointed a bright red fingernail at Shandra.

"I don't know what you're talking about," Shandra said, feeling the hair on the back of her neck bristling.

The woman laughed. "You'll know soon enough." She tugged on Doring's arm. "Come on, Sugar, I'm starving."

The two wandered off with their heads together whispering.

Shandra didn't feel like eating anymore. A lump of dread settled in her stomach.

Ryan grasped her hand. "Don't worry. They're just trying to draw attention away from themselves."

She couldn't shake the despair engulfing her. "What lies do you think that woman told the state police?"

"It's hard to say. I'll call in a favor from a stater I know and see what kind of nonsense she told them." Ryan squeezed her hand. "Come on, we came here for a nice dinner and to see those two. They are pretty chummy for Ms. Vincent having just lost a lover."

"She doesn't strike me as the kind to fall in love. She's a user like Carl." Shandra glanced over at the table where the two sat close, acting like love birds. "She wants something from Sidney. That's why she's hanging on his arm and probably sleeping in his bed."

"Perhaps it's an alibi. Though I have both their

comments from the first day saying they were both alone at the time of the shooting." He sat back as the waiter set their food in front of them. "Eat up. I heard they have a live band in the bar during the ski season. I thought we'd check it out."

Shandra wasn't sure she wanted to dance the night away, but it was better than going home and worrying.

Chapter Ten

Ryan enjoyed holding Shandra in his arms as they danced to the jazzy tunes of the band. The lead singer's voice was smooth and warm. After two hours, he drove Shandra home, kissing her goodnight at her bedroom door.

Now he sat in the guest room reading the responses from the emails he'd sent out earlier in the day. There were several assaults and restraining orders against Landers, leading him to request more information on the women and their families, particularly the men who had assaulted Landers.

Clicking through the files, his finger paused on the mouse and he stared at a photo. One of the men in question looked a lot like the lead singer from the band at the lodge bar.

He clicked to open the file on the man named Woody York. York had attacked Landers after a gallery showing. When the officers hauled Woody to the station, he stated Landers had been keeping his sister,

Shelly York, from her family and she had become despondent and shut off.

If Carl Landers wasn't already dead, Ryan would have felt the need to throw the man in a cell with a bunch of sex offenders. From the reports he read, Landers had ruined many women's lives.

He typed in Shelly York's last known address, hoping to contact her.

***

Shandra stood in a blizzard. Snow whipped around her, holding her prisoner in a white world. She used swimming motions to move through the wind and snow. Something in the distance glowed and the howling of the wind turned to music. Carl stood on stage, pointing toward the jazz singer she'd enjoyed at the lodge. The man's face was scrunched in anger as he raised his guitar, bashing Carl over the head. A young woman stood off to the side. Tears glistened in her eyes, brighter than the lights beaming down on the two men. Shandra drew her gaze from the woman and scoured the scene for the pistol. "It has to be here! It has to be here!"

"Shandra? Shandra, are you okay?"

She sat up, pushed her hair off her face and stared at Sheba, standing by the door wagging her tail. Pounding came again on the door.

"Ryan?"

The knob turned. Ryan stepped through, his face wrinkled with worry. "Were you dreaming?" He sat on the side of the bed and put a hand on her face.

"Yes." She relayed the dream and gazed up at him. "What does it mean?"

Ryan pulled her into his arms and held her against

his chest. "The singer's name is Woody York, and his sister was one of Landers' conquests. He was arrested for assaulting Landers."

"He didn't kill Carl," she said, pushing out of the warm, comforting embrace.

"How do you know?" Ryan studied her so intently her cheeks heated under his scrutiny.

"There wasn't a pistol in my dream. But I think we need to return to the lodge and talk with Woody. It seems a bit coincidental that he was working at the lodge where Carl was vacationing." Shandra's heart had stopped racing. Her world was coming into a clearer focus.

"I agree. I'd planned to take you back there tonight after reading the arrest reports." Ryan slid his hand up and down her arm. "Sure you're okay now?"

"Yeah. Sometimes these dreams seem so real." She hoped they didn't find evidence against Woody. He was a talented musician.

Ryan leaned forward and kissed her.

She leaned into the kiss, enjoying the way it made her feel safe and cared for.

He pulled back with a groan. "See you in the morning." He stood and walked out of the room.

Shandra sighed. One of these days, she'd invite him to stay. But not until this mess was over.

***

Ryan finished putting away the snowshoes he and Shandra used that morning for a walk in the woods. As he walked out of the barn, he noticed a dark blue SUV parked in front of Shandra's house. There were lights hidden inside the front window of the vehicle. An unmarked detective vehicle. The state police had arrived to question her.

Knowing Shandra was working in the studio, Ryan headed there. He entered the building and discovered two plain-clothed officers standing inside the door, while Shandra stood beside her wheel. The one closest to Shandra turned and Ryan's anxiety lowered.

"Pete, glad to see you're on the case," he said, holding out a hand to the tall, sandy-haired man in jeans and a blue ski coat.

"Greer. Heard you'd been sidelined on this one." The man's gaze drifted between Shandra and Ryan. "I see why."

The need to stand up for Shandra was too strong. He couldn't stop the words. "I would have treated this case as unbiased as any other case. That Shandra and I are friends doesn't change the fact she didn't kill Landers."

The officer he didn't know smiled. "Unbiased?"

Shandra stepped forward. "Ryan is saying that I didn't even know Carl Landers was here until I heard about his death. From the time I arrived at the Coeur d'Alene airport until Ryan received the call about a body on the ski run, he and I had been together."

Pete narrowed his gaze at Ryan. "This true? You were with her the whole time?"

"I've been at this ranch since picking her up and until dispatch called me to the mountain." They didn't need to know he and Shandra weren't sleeping together.

"I'd like to discuss some information we've discovered about Ms. Higheagle and the deceased." Pete clearly wanted him to leave the studio.

"Ryan knows all about my past with Carl. There's no need to send him away." Shandra switched off the pottery wheel and wiped her hands on a rag that hung from her pocket. "How about we all go in the house and I'll make some coffee?"

Pete and the other officer shared a glance then nodded.

"I could use a cup of coffee," Pete said.

The back door of the studio slammed open. "Shandra, the feds are here!" shouted Lil, stepping into the studio.

The two staters had their guns in their hands.

"Lil, they aren't feds, they are state policemen." Shandra waved to the door. "Close the door. We're going in the house for some coffee. Why don't you see if the coasters we glazed are ready to go in the kiln?"

"Put your guns away. This is Shandra's employee." Ryan walked to the front door and held it open for Shandra and the two staters to exit. When the three were halfway to the house, he turned back to Lil. "Outbursts like that will make those men think Shandra has something to hide."

Lil glared at him. "Takes a snake to know a snake."

He shook his head and followed the three into the house. After closing the door, Ryan walked over to the officer he didn't know. "Ryan Greer, Weippe County Detective. And you are?"

"Stu Whorter."

"Stu. Good to meet you." Ryan took the other stool along the counter and watched Shandra fill the coffee maker with water and measure the grounds. They'd finished off a pot that morning before their snowshoe trek.

"Ms. Higheagle, according to one of our sources, you once lived with Carl Landers." Pete studied

Shandra.

Ryan was aware of Stu's gaze on him. He kept his features as stony as if he were doing the interrogating.

Shandra flicked the switch on the coffee maker and turned to face them. "Yes, when I was a college student, Professor Landers swept me off my innocent feet. It wasn't until he'd taken away my fight and spirit that I'd realized what he'd done. He'd made me a possession that he manipulated."

Pete jotted a note in the book in front of him. "So when you left, was it amicable?"

"Amicable? No." She let out a ragged laugh. "He refused to let me go and threatened me. I hired an attorney after he broke into my apartment and she helped me get a restraining order. When I graduated and left New Mexico, I hadn't seen or heard from him until I was there this past weekend."

"What did you talk about when you saw him this past weekend?" Pete's gaze never left Shandra's face.

"Nothing. I avoided him. I didn't want him making a scene and ruining the event for everyone who put it on." She turned to the cupboards and plucked four cups from the shelf.

"You saw him but didn't speak to him? Didn't invite him to come to Huckleberry?" Pete's tone reflected he didn't believe her.

Shandra spun around. Her face was red, her eyes narrowed. "I didn't want to speak to the man, and I did not invite him to Huckleberry." Her lips curled in disgust. "I never wanted to see the man again."

"Then why did he insist on coming here for a ski vacation after seeing you?" Stu asked.

"I don't know. Ask the woman who came here

with him. She'd have more of an idea than I would since I've not spoken to the man in nine years." Shandra filled the coffee mugs.

Ryan was impressed that her hands didn't shake as she poured the coffee.

She placed a cup in front of each of the staters, and then placed one in front of him.

"We did talk with Tabitha Vincent. She said Landers came here at your request." Pete put his pen down and picked up the coffee mug.

"She's lying," Shandra said in a deep, menacing tone. "I never once talked with Carl. I didn't even know he was here until I heard about his death."

"How did you hear about his death?" Stu asked.

She turned her attention to Stu. "Ryan's note saying he had a body on the mountain and then Lil said she heard on the radio a professor from a New Mexico college had died on the mountain. I still didn't know it was Carl until I spoke with Ryan."

"How did you feel when you heard it was Carl Landers?" Pete asked.

"That's not a fair question," Ryan butt in. They had no right to try to put words into Shandra's mouth.

"It's okay." She put a hand on Ryan's arm. "I was relieved. I wouldn't have to worry about running into him again and feeling like a victim. But I was also sorry. He had family that loved him and no one should lose a loved one by violence."

Ryan knew she was thinking about her own father who she'd recently discovered had been murdered by her stepfather.

Chapter Eleven

Shandra really hoped the two policemen would leave soon. She couldn't think of any more questions they could ask her. And she felt all her answers had been clear that she didn't kill the man.

The officer named Pete flipped through the notepad in front of him. "You say you were relieved. Was that because the tapes he had on you wouldn't get made public?"

Her blood chilled, and her heart stopped in her chest. "W-what tapes? I thought that woman only said that to try and hurt me."

Ryan shot to his feet. "Have you found any tapes or are you just going on the word of a woman who has been in and out of jail for scams and cons the last ten years?"

Stu stood up beside Ryan as if he planned to grab him.

Pete raised his hand, motioning for both men to sit. "How do you know so much about Ms. Vincent?" He leveled a gaze on Ryan.

"After her accusations in the diner, I felt she wasn't Landers usual type. So I made some inquiries."

Shandra stared at Ryan. He'd sent off lots of emails, but he hadn't told her about Tabby. What else had he learned that he was keeping from her?

"Unofficially?" Pete asked.

"Yes, unofficially." Ryan stepped around the counter and stood beside her. "I won't have you building a case against Shandra when I know she didn't do it."

She liked the solidarity he showed.

A thump sounded on the back door and Shandra moved to the door, letting Sheba in. The dog's belly and legs were covered with snowballs.

"I need to clean the snow off my dog," she said, pointing to the laundry room. Sheba hung her head but headed into the shower.

"That's a big dog. I bet its foot prints are the size of the ones found near the body," Pete said, making himself heard clear into the laundry room with the water running.

Shandra grit her teeth. She wasn't commenting. She and Sheba were nowhere near that ski run. They hadn't traveled more than half a mile due to the deep snow. Turning from the shower to grab a towel, she caught a glimpse of Stu standing in the laundry room door.

"There isn't a way out of here, and I wouldn't try to run anyway. I'm innocent and have no reason to be bullied by you or your partner." She toweled off the dog, then pointed toward the other room. "Go to the fire."

Sheba bounded past Stu, who had to back out of

the door or be flattened.

Shandra dropped the towel in the hamper and headed into the kitchen. She noted everyone had empty coffee cups. A good cue for them to leave.

"If you have no more questions, I'd like to get back to work." She stood by the back door with her hand on the knob.

"Ms. Higheagle do you own a twenty-two caliber gun?" Pete didn't look like he planned to move from the stool any time soon.

"No. I have a thirty-eight rifle that I carry with me when I ride in the woods. It's hanging up in Lil's room. Would you like to see it?" she asked.

"A single woman like yourself doesn't keep a pistol in the house for protection?" Stu asked.

Shandra glared at him. "No, I do not. The only reason I carry the rifle when I ride is to scare off cougars and bears. I would never shoot at them. If someone comes into my house, I will knock them out or hide and call the police. I would never kill any creature." She crossed her arms. Her stepfather had tried to get her to kill deer but she couldn't. They didn't need the meat, they butchered cattle. There wasn't any sense in killing something when you weren't going to use it for anything other than a trophy mount.

"I guess your big dog would protect you," Pete said.

Shandra and Ryan both chuckled.

"Sheba might be big, but she's more like the cowardly lion in the *Wizard of Oz*. She tends to hide when there is anything scary," Ryan said.

"That large dog?" Stu said with skepticism.

"Yes. If a gun goes off, she runs to me or under

whatever she can find and lays down on her belly."
Shandra always found it comical.

"Which means if Shandra had been on the ski run
with Sheba and a gun, if a twenty-two had gone off, the
dog would have flattened to the ground and there would
have been distinct marks." Ryan picked up the empty
cups and set them in the sink. "I think you've
uncovered all the answers you need."

Pete finally stood. He studied Ryan, then headed
for the back door. Before exiting, he turned. "Don't
leave town. You're still a suspect."

She nodded but was relieved the men were leaving.
"I don't have plans to go anywhere. I have work to do."

Pete nodded and opened the door. He walked out.
Stu shot a glance from her to Ryan and back to her and
followed his partner out the door.

Shandra crossed the room and closed the door. The
wind was picking up, and it looked like they were in for
more snow.

"Do you think they believed me?" she asked,
watching as the men walked to the front of the house
where their SUV was parked.

Ryan wrapped his arms around her. "We cleared up
some things, and gave them more to think about."

"Why didn't you tell me about Tabby being in and
out of jail?" She continued to stare out the window.

"I received the information this morning while you
were out working in the studio and hadn't had time to
tell you." Ryan turned her. "She is a con artist. I would
bet if we asked to see the videos she keeps talking
about, you wouldn't be on them. I have a feeling when
she became close with Landers, she discovered tapes he
may have made after you and has been blackmailing the

women involved. Now that she knows you were one of his lovers, she probably thinks there are videos. You are a perceptive person. I think you would have known if he had been videotaping you."

"I was a mess back then. I don't know if I would've known." That was the part that scared her the most. There could be videos and that would be a powerful motive for her to have killed Carl. Especially now that her career was taking off.

"Where do you think he'd keep the videos?" Ryan asked, leading her to the counter and making another pot of coffee.

"I don't want any more coffee, my stomach is aching from what I've had. I'll take some herbal tea, please." She thought on what he'd asked. Even though she'd lived with Carl, he'd been a secretive man and only told or showed her what he wanted her to know. "I wonder if Carl still lived in the house on the edge of town. It was a small adobe house. Cute, with a southwestern charm. He had a housekeeper. She would know where he might keep things he considered valuable."

Ryan placed a cup of tea in front of her. "What was the housekeeper's name?"

Shandra thought back to the first time Carl took her to his house. He'd introduced her to the woman. "Mrs. Martinez." She conjured up the woman's small stature, round smiling face, and apron over polyester top and pants. "Ramona Martinez. Why?"

"I'll contact a private investigator to see Mrs. Martinez and ask her where Landers kept his valuables. If we can get our hands on any tapes that might be there, we can discover if you were taped or not. That would be one less motive and one less reason to fear what Ms. Vincent has to say. If we can prove she is lying about that, then her other accusations will be considered coming from a liar."

She liked this idea except for… "What if there are tapes? We'll have to hand them over to the authorities."

"We will. It will be our good faith gesture that we aren't worried about the tapes coming out." Ryan reached across the counter, placing his hand on hers. "There are many people in government positions with scandals in their history. Being young and innocent, you couldn't stop a man like Landers from exploiting you. People will understand."

"I hope you're right." She was glad her father and grandmother weren't here to learn about this. "I need to call Aunt Jo and tell her what's going on. I don't want them to learn about my past from the newspapers."

"Go call her. I'll find a private investigator in Albuquerque." Ryan watched as Shandra walked out of the room. She'd started the day so strong. One round of questioning with the State Police and she was starting to lose that strength. As a county detective he didn't usually think highly of private investigators, but he had used a few back in Chicago when they needed information unofficially to catch a bad guy. He felt hiring a P.I. to find out if there were tapes was well worth the money. This way, he and Shandra would be ahead of any more questions and accusations about the tapes.

Chapter Twelve

That evening Ryan took Shandra to her favorite Italian restaurant, Rigatoni. She hugged Miranda Aducci, the daughter of the owner, and was glad the woman didn't ask her any questions about the murder.

Miranda hugged Ryan to her tall, voluptuous body and winked at Shandra. "It makes my family happy to see you and Ryan are still seeing one another."

"Thank you. I'm happy to have found a man who cares enough to wait me out." She flashed Ryan a smile.

He grasped her hand. "I don't plan on going anywhere any time soon. You're worth waiting for."

"Oh my!" Miranda fanned her face. "I would think you two are Italians the way you go on like such love birds." The bell over the door jingled. "Decide what you would like to drink. I will be back."

Shandra giggled. Miranda and her family were some of the first people in Huckleberry to welcome her. She loved eating the Italian food and feeling like family when she visited the restaurant.

"We could have wine. We're only driving as far as the lodge and there we can drink sodas or tea," Ryan suggested.

"I would love a glass of wine with my dinner." She stared out the window. Miranda had given them a secluded table that faced the window showing off the lighted runs on the mountain. She shivered, wondering where on the runs Carl had met his end.

"Cold?" Ryan asked.

"No. I'll just never be able to look at the mountain and not wonder who killed Carl up there." She focused her attention on Ryan. "As despicable as he was, no one should die from the hand of another."

"We'll discover who did it and get justice." He fiddled with his napkin, putting it on his lap, and then folding and putting it back under his utensils.

"Why are you nervous?" she asked.

"I don't like how long it's taking the P.I. to gather information on the house and tapes."

Miranda arrived with a bottle of white wine. "I know this is your favorite," she said, smiling at Shandra.

"You read my mind. Thank you." She held out the wine glass sitting on the table.

Miranda poured a quarter of a glass and waited for her to try the golden liquid.

"It's perfect!" Shandra said, holding her glass up to be filled.

The hostess filled Ryan's glass and placed the bottle on the table in an ice bucket. She knew Shandra preferred her wine ice cold.

"Have you decided on your meal?" Miranda asked.

"We'll take two of the specials," Shandra said, feeling bold ordering for Ryan.

He nodded and Miranda headed to the kitchen with their order.

"What is the special tonight?" Ryan asked.

"I don't know but everything here is good." She sipped her wine, savoring the mellow fruit flavors. The last couple of days had set her nerves on end. Tonight, they would talk with the singer in the band at the lodge and see if he could be a suspect instead of her.

Ryan's phone buzzed. He glanced at the screen and nodded. "It's the P.I. I'm going to step outside and take this."

Shandra felt a rock lodge in her throat. She hoped the man had found nothing, but at the same time, if there were tapes, she wanted to get a hold of them.

He put his coat on and kissed her head. "It's going to be fine."

She watched his back as he walked through the restaurant and out the front door.

Ryan walked around the corner of the building so he could keep an eye on Shandra and she could see him.

"Were you able to talk to the housekeeper?" he asked, Ed Aldo, the private investigator he'd hired.

"Yes. She had just learned of Professor Landers' death. She was shook up but answered the questions without hesitation."

"Good. Did you learn anything?" He hoped there were no tapes and that Tabitha Vincent was pulling a scam.

"She showed me where the professor had many tapes in a closet. I scanned the labels, none had the name you gave me. But there were five missing."

Ryan didn't like that. Was Shandra on one of them?

"Did you write down the names on the tapes that were there?" His plan was to track down the ones who had battled with Landers after the splits. And who had family members assault Landers.

"Yes. I will email my report and the names to you tonight." Ed had come highly recommended by a friend in the Albuquerque police department.

"Thank you. You didn't happen to ask the housekeeper if anyone had been there since Landers left?"

"She said only the sister. She knocked on the door asking for Carl. Discovered he was on a trip and left."

Landers' sister. "When was this?"

"The day he headed to Idaho."

This information could be helpful. She could have followed him to Huckleberry. "Thanks. Send me a bill with the information."

"I will. It was a pleasure working for you."

The phone went dead. He glanced up and found Shandra peering out the window at him. He smiled, tucked the phone in his coat pocket, and hurried back into the warm building.

Miranda placed their plates on the table as Ryan approached.

"You were gone and didn't eat your salad," she reprimanded.

"I'll eat it along with my dinner. Thank you." He shed his coat and hung it on the hook on the wall by their table.

"Anything else?" the waitress asked.

"We're fine. Thank you," Shandra said, pushing

85

her salad around with her fork. From the plate full of lettuce, she hadn't eaten a bite of her salad.

Miranda left and Shandra leaned across the table. "What did your friend have to say?"

Ryan had hoped to avoid this until after they ate. He didn't think either one would have an appetite when he told her the news. "You have to promise you will eat after I tell you everything."

She put her fork down. "That means there were tapes."

"Yes, but none with your name on them. The housekeeper was helpful to the P.I. and showed him the closet of tapes. He wrote down all the names. But he also noticed there were five missing."

Shandra picked up her wine and gulped several swallows. "Mine?"

"We don't know. The woman didn't read the names, just knew they were in there from when she cleaned."

"You would have thought she'd have been curious if one of the names matched a girl she knew had lived with him." Shandra sloshed the golden liquid in the glass and took a sip.

The contents of the glass was going down faster than Ryan liked. He reached over and took the glass from her. "Eat something before that wine hits your empty stomach."

She nodded and pushed the food around on her plate.

"Did the P.I. say anything else?" She put a bite of veal into her mouth and chewed.

"Yes. It seems the sister came by the day Landers left for here. The housekeeper told her where he'd gone."

"Alexis went by his house? That doesn't sound like her. She avoided his 'den of depravity' at all costs." Shandra stabbed another piece of meat.

"She knew what he did to college co-eds?"

"I'm not sure how, but I answered the phone a couple of times when she'd called. Her language and tone made it clear she found her brother revolting. And she knew what he was doing to us." She shuddered. "It's amazing when I think back. There had to be faculty who knew what he was doing. I went from an A student to a barely C while living with Carl. I know my appearance had become frightful because I lost so much weight, hoping he'd toss me to the side and move on." She cut more meat and ate with gusto.

Ryan smiled. At least she was eating to counter the wine she'd drank. "It does seem odd that the faculty after all these years of restraining orders and even the assaults wouldn't have given him the boot."

"I know several of the board members came over for a card night. Carl always gave me movie tickets those nights." Her eyes narrowed. "Do you think they were watching the videos and not playing cards? He always said he'd set up the card table after I left, and it would be put away when I returned." She dropped her fork and splayed her fingers across her face. "Do you think he showed…?"

The tips of her ears were bright red. Ryan reached across, pulling her hands from her face. "Shandra, you had no control over what that man did. And if there were others who let him get away with it, we'll make sure they are punished too. I told Ed, the P.I., to tell the police about the tapes, that they might be evidence in the homicide."

Her head snapped up, and she stared into his eyes. "But those other women? How can you drag their reputations through this?"

"I have their names and plan to start calling each of them tomorrow. If they know about the tapes, then someone, Ms. Vincent most likely, was blackmailing them. They should be happy the authorities have the tapes and she can no longer extort money."

"And if they don't know about the tapes?" Shandra picked up her wine and gulped again.

He reached across the table and set the glass down. "I'll explain it to them and let them know the tapes are part of the homicide investigation by the police."

"I wonder how many others were like me and hadn't a clue he'd taped us while he belittled us." Her golden eyes grew dark and stormy. "If he were still alive, I'm not sure what I would do to him if I saw him."

"You'd give him an earful and bring criminal charges against him." Ryan grasped her hand. Time to make her think of something else. "What did your aunt have to say when you called her?"

Shandra picked up a piece of asparagus on her fork. "She said Grandmother had a feeling things were wrong with me, but didn't want to interfere. She knew I would find my medicine and come out strong." She stared at the vegetable. "If I had known Ella knew what was happening, I would have been mortified and probably tried to break away sooner. I didn't think anyone cared. When I tried to talk to my mother about it, she said a college professor wouldn't treat students that way, especially ones who he loved." She set the fork down. "Carl did not love me or any of the women. He used us to torture and fill some sadistic need he had. He preyed on our innocence, and when he had us hooked, he became a domineering pervert."

She picked the fork back up and stabbed a spear of asparagus.

Ryan couldn't fathom what all Shandra had been exposed to by the man. But he understood her fear of taking their relationship to a more intimate level.

"Let's not talk about this anymore and finish this dinner. After dinner we'll concentrate on Woody York and not what the P.I. found." He picked up his glass of wine and held it out to toast.

Shandra clinked her glass to his. "I can't believe you are sticking by me after learning about my sordid past."

"Our pasts are what make us who we are today. I care about you and wouldn't want you any other way." He sipped his wine and dug into his dinner. The sooner they arrived at the lodge bar, the sooner they could corner Woody and talk to him about his sister.

Chapter Thirteen

The wine had mellowed Shandra. She sat in the lounge, swaying to the soft jazz music as the band performed an instrumental piece. While she wasn't happy to learn there could still be tapes out there, she was ready to discover more about the lead singer. His sister had been one of Carl's conquests. The singer's dark hair was cropped close to his head. He wore a T-shirt, blue jeans, and sneakers. She'd guess his sister would have lived with Carl after Shandra left college.

"Let's dance." Ryan stood and held out his hand.

She smiled. She'd only danced with him at his brother's wedding until last night. Dancing with him every night could become addicting. Grasping his outstretched hand, she stood and followed him onto the floor.

Ryan pulled her into his arms.

Shandra sighed and rested her head on his shoulder as the slow strains melted her inhibitions. His strong arms were reassuring. He'd stuck with her through so much, and while her past was nothing to be proud of, he worked to dig it up to keep her from being accused of murder.

The song stopped.

"We'll take a fifteen-minute break," Woody York announced.

"That's our cue." Ryan stepped away from her but retained her hand. He walked over to the end of the bar where the band had gathered.

"My girlfriend and I really like your music." Ryan held up a five-dollar bill, catching Woody's attention. "We'd like to buy you a drink and have you come talk to us." Ryan nodded toward their table, not far from the where the band was set up.

The man's face lit up. "I always make time for fans and a drink." Woody motioned to the bartender with a half-full glass of amber liquid. "Bring another of these over to this couple's table."

Shandra followed Ryan to their table and took the seat next to him. Woody sat across from them.

"You like our music? We have CDs for sale at the bar." Woody gulped down the rest of his drink as the bartender brought over his second glass.

Ryan paid for the drink and smiled at Woody.

Shandra decided to let him do the talking. He knew how to get information out of people.

"How did you come to be playing at this lodge?" he asked.

Woody grinned. "Our manager called us up last week and said the original band scheduled to play here had to cancel and could we get here by Friday. This time of year a lodge is one of the best gigs. Skiers are here to have a good time, and they don't mind tipping the band. Also, ski resorts tend to throw in free skiing as part of the payment."

"So this wasn't originally on your schedule?" Ryan picked up his glass of iced tea.

Woody glanced from Ryan to her, his eyes narrowing suspiciously. "What's this about? I wouldn't think a fan would care that we squeaked into this gig."

"It's interesting that the man you attacked four years ago was found dead on this ski slope while you are here." Ryan sipped his tea.

Shandra picked her drink up and studied Woody's reaction.

Woody sat up straighter. "How do you know about me going off on that professor? Who are you?"

"I'm with the Weippe County Sheriff. We were sorry to hear about your sister, Shelly."

"I don't talk about my sister." Woody rose from his chair.

Ryan grasped his wrist. "Why did she take her own life?"

Shandra's gaze flew to Ryan. He hadn't told her this. She had to jump in. "Did Professor Landers abuse her?"

Woody stared at her. "What do you know about her life with Landers?"

"I know how he treated me. What a monster he was, and how it took all of my strength to get away from him." Her spine straightened as the power she'd felt once she left Carl came surging back to her. "I can only imagine what happened to her."

"Did he tape tying you up and humiliating you?" Woody's low, simmering tone revealed his rage. He slowly lowered back onto the chair.

"I didn't think so, but now that we're learning about tapes and other women…" She shook her head. "I honestly don't know."

"No one tried to blackmail you about tapes?" Woody asked.

"No. I don't know if they didn't get around to me or if he started videoing after I left." She put a hand on Woody's arm. "Is that what happened to your sister? Was she contacted to pay or the tapes would be sent to someone?"

"Yes. Shelly was already a mess, drinking, drugs, living like a hermit from what that man did to her. When she received the call about exposing the tapes, she didn't know what to think. She didn't even know he'd filmed her. When money was demanded, she didn't know what to do. She didn't have a job or any money to pay. She refused to take any from me, and feared our parents would find out. She said the only way to not be blackmailed was to be dead." He held his head in his hands. "I didn't think she meant it until the police informed my parents she'd overdosed."

"Is that when you assaulted Landers?" Ryan asked.

Woody's face turned a deep red and his veins bulged on his forehead. "That was the second time. The first time is when he pressed charges. When I beat him up to get Shelly away from him. She'd told me all about the things he'd made her do."

"When I confronted him the second time, I demanded he give me the tapes on my sister. That he'd killed her by blackmailing her. He laughed at me. Told me my sister must have made up all those tales." Woody fisted his hands. "That's when I hit him. Knocked him down and beat on him until he was

93

unconscious. Then I went through his house and found the tapes." He shook his head. "If I'd have been thinking straight I would have taken all the tapes so he couldn't blackmail anyone else. But I only took the tapes he had of Shelly. I didn't even look at them." Woody lifted a trembling hand and took a sip from his drink. "I took them out into the desert, started a fire, and threw them in."

"Did you see Landers here?" Ryan asked, drawing the conversation back to what they needed to know. He felt sorry for Woody, but he could be the person responsible for Landers' death.

"Couldn't miss him. That woman he was with laughed loud and drew everyone's attention. Even Mr. Doring's." Woody shook his head. "She acted like she wanted the two old geezers to fight over her."

Musical instruments being tuned caught Woody's attention. He glanced over his shoulder to where the band had gathered once again. "Gotta go." He stood, then turned back around. "I didn't kill him, but he and Doring sat here talking long after that blonde left the bar the night he died."

Ryan studied him as he walked back to the band. He didn't act like a person with something to hide.

"You know, we thought Doring killed his wife. He does have a temper," Shandra said, cutting into his thoughts.

"I questioned him before I was tossed off the case. While he doesn't have a tight alibi, he has one. This lodge has key cards that register when someone goes in and out of the rooms. He was in his room before the time of death and didn't come out until the morning."

Shandra tapped a finger against her drink glass.

"And he does live on the top floor and would have to come out his door to use the stairs. Now where are we?"

"The only other person who knew Landers before is Ms. Vincent." Ryan sipped his iced tea.

"And she had access to his pistol," added Shandra.

"We have to find that weapon." He stared at the door. Doring and Ms. Vincent entered the bar. Just who they needed to watch, but he didn't want a scene. "Let's dance." He drew Shandra out onto the dance floor, maneuvering them through the middle of the dancers and to the far side as he kept an eye on Doring and Ms. Vincent.

"Why are we covering so much of the floor?" Shandra asked.

"To stay out of Doring and Ms. Vincent's view but to watch them."

Her body tensed and her feet fumbled.

"Don't worry, I have you." He kissed her temple and watched the couple.

Doring had his hands all over the younger woman, making him look like a perverted old man. Ms. Vincent laughed and placed her hand on his leg close to the man's crotch.

Ryan shuddered.

"What's wrong?" Shandra asked, whispering in his ear.

"Watching those two makes me want to be sprayed with disinfectant."

She laughed softly.

"They're coming onto the dance floor. I'll start moving us toward the door."

As the song ended, he grasped Shandra's hand,

leading her off the floor, to their table to collect their coats, and out the door into the lobby.

"Thank you! I didn't want to have that woman shouting lies again," Shandra said, as he helped her put her coat on.

"We won't learn anything from her. I think I'll have the P.I. look into her background more." He led Shandra to the door and stopped when he spotted Pete and Stu, the two State Police Detectives, headed into the lodge.

"Come on," He tugged Shandra to the side of the lobby and pulled her into his arms, kissing her. He barely registered the two men's footsteps passing as he enjoyed the kiss. Slowly, he drew away and smiled. "That's the best way I've ever avoided someone."

Shandra stared at him. "What do you mean?"

"The two state detectives were headed in here. I figured they didn't need to know we were investigating ourselves. I made us disappear."

"I didn't know you were a magician." She licked her lips. "But you do have some magic in those lips."

He laughed. "Come on, let's get out of here."

They left the lodge, even though, he would have loved to be a spider on the wall in the bar to see who the staters questioned.

Chapter Fourteen

Shandra went to bed feeling peaceful for the first time since her trip to New Mexico. It could have been the wine or the kiss, she wasn't sure which, but she felt lighter and freer than she had in a very long time.

Sheba settled at the end of her bed with a grumble. Shandra patted her head and turned out the light. Her thoughts bounced between Ryan and Carl as sleep overtook her.

Ella waved her arms in a gathering motion. Shandra thought it meant for her to come to her grandmother, but a wind pushed her back. "What do you want, Grandmother?" she asked. Ella continued the motion. "What do you want me to gather? Evidence? I'm trying."

Wispy visions of her father, Aunt Jo, and other family members appeared in Ella's arms.

"Family? I need to gather family? Whose family? Carl? The women he exploited?"

Ella opened her arms. Her family disappeared, as

97

well as Ella.

*Shandra spun in a circle. "Where do I start and
with who?" The dream left her with more questions and
no answers.*

***

Ryan rose early, made coffee, and opened his
computer. Technology had made gathering information
so much easier. He opened the list of women who had
sought restraining orders and injunctions against
Landers. It appeared they were all after Shandra left
Landers. She'd started something or the women after
her got wise sooner.

As he read through the court records, Dana
Benham's name popped up as the person accompanying
the women through the paperwork.

Shandra wandered into the kitchen sniffing.
"Coffee. It's such a wonderful smell in the morning.
Thank you for making it." She touched his shoulder and
continued to the coffee maker.

"What was the name of the attorney who helped
you with the injunction against Landers?" he asked, and
raised his cup of coffee to his lips.

She poured a mug of coffee and turned to him.
"Dana. Dana Benham. She was the legal aid for an
abuse shelter." She sat on a stool next to him and
scooted close.

"I was looking up the other women who had
restraining orders against Landers. They were all
represented by Ms. Benham." He peered into her eyes.
"That seems highly unlikely to be a coincidence."

She shook her head. "Not if the women were like
me and went to the police first. The shelter Dana
represented was recommended to me by the police."

Ryan glanced at the time on his computer. Most of the women lived in the Pacific or Central time zones. It was only seven. He'd wait an hour and start calling. The women were the key to who killed Landers. He had a gut feeling it had to do with the videos.

"Ready for me to make breakfast?" he asked, needing something to do while he waited an hour.

Shandra rose from her stool. "You don't have to make breakfast, you already made coffee."

"It will give me something to do until I can start making calls." He put his hands on her shoulders. They hadn't talked about the long kiss he'd pulled her into while trying to avoid Pete and Stu the night before. The drive home had been quiet, and they'd parted with him kissing her good-night at her bedroom door. Living in the same house but treating it like they had separate apartments was getting old. But he understood why Shandra was taking their relationship slow. Her last one had been ripped out of a T.V. crime drama. And he really shouldn't hook his name to anyone until he was sure he couldn't be connected to the take down of the most feared gang in Chicago.

He leaned down, kissed her lips, and pulled back, smiling. "I could get used to this every morning."

Her cheeks darkened and her eyes flashed with interest. "I could too."

He stared into her eyes. "Do you mean that?"

She nodded and a tentative grin tipped her lips.

His heart thumped in his chest. "It's good to know that wall you built up is slowly crumbling."

"I have nothing to do with it. The crumbling is all you."

His phone buzzed, breaking the moment. He

glanced at the screen. "It's Cathleen."

He swiped his finger across the phone and answered. "What do you have, Cathleen?"

"They found the murder weapon."

"That's good news." He grinned at Shandra.

"Not really. They found it under a tree east of the murder site with a rag wrapped around it. The rag had traces of clay and was sent to the forensics lab." Cathleen covered the phone and spoke to someone. "I have to go. Thought you should know. You'll probably have visitors when the results come back on the rag."

"Thank you for calling." He hit the off button and stared out the kitchen window. How did he tell Shandra she was still the main suspect?

"What did Cathleen have to say? Was it about the investigation?" She put a hand on his arm.

"They found the murder weapon."

"That's good! They'll be able to discover where it came from and get the killer." She started digging food out of the refrigerator.

Ryan walked over and stood beside Shandra. He grasped her shoulders and turned her to face him. "It's not good. The weapon was found wrapped in a clay covered rag under a tree east of the murder site."

Her eyes flashed with fear and her body wobbled. "I didn't do it. Who is laying all this out to look like me?"

"I don't know. But it's clear they are trying to throw blame on you. You're smart enough you would never wrap a murder weapon in a rag that would give you away." Ryan pulled her into his arms. "We'll figure this out. Who has access to your studio? That has to be where they got the rag."

"Me, you, Lil, anyone who comes to visit. The two State Police Detectives were in there. But they are the only people I know of lately other than us."

"Do you lock the studio?" He was pretty sure she didn't, living so far from anyone else on a secluded road.

"No. But Lil or I are here all the time. We'd see if someone came." Her eyes no longer showed fear, they sparked with anger.

"Not if they came through the woods and snuck in the back door of the studio. But they'd have to have knowledge of your studio." He pulled out the pans needed to make breakfast. "Of the people we consider suspects, who has been out here to your studio?"

Shandra cracked eggs and started clicking off the suspects. "I know Tabby and Woody haven't been here. As for the other women or relatives of them, I wouldn't know until I see them. I give tours of my studio during the art week in June." She stopped and stared at him. "Sidney Doring came out here during one of those tours." Her anger ratcheted up a notch. He'd assaulted her at the last summer art event, and she'd pressed charges. She could see him killing a man to get the woman and framing her.

Ryan shoved crumbled sausage around in the pan. "He couldn't have known about the pistol unless Landers had it on him when they met on the slope. He could have shot Landers, somehow managed those incriminating footprints and carried the weapon back with him and set it up to be found later."

"But how did he know about my connection to Carl? It would be ridiculous to pin the murder on me if I didn't have a connection to the man." She handed

Ryan the bowl of whipped eggs and leaned against the counter, watching him cook. "Do you think Sidney and Tabby worked together? Tabby might have known about me. I'm sure there had to be talk among the university staff when Carl came to my show."

"They didn't have much time to put a plan together since Landers and Ms. Vincent arrived on Tuesday, and he was killed Tuesday night." Ryan slid the concoction from the pan onto the plates she'd placed on the counter.

"Sidney helping or killing Carl makes no sense. As far as we know Sidney and Carl hadn't met until in the bar at the ski lodge. And I really don't see Sidney killing Carl over a women. There are plenty of them at the ski lodge right now." Shandra took one of the plates and dug eating utensils out of a drawer. She sat at the counter and handed a set to Ryan.

"None of this makes sense." He grabbed the coffee pot, refilling both their cups.

"We probably have a day, maybe two, before they get the results of the rag they found with the weapon." He sat down. "At eight I'll start calling the other women and hopefully by the time Pete and Stu come back to question you about the rag, we'll have other suspects for them to contact."

Shandra scooped up a bite and nodded her head. It would really break her spirit if she were convicted of killing Carl. He would have finally won his sadistic need for power over her.

Chapter Fifteen

Ryan took his computer and phone into the main room as soon as he and Shandra had cleaned up from breakfast. He wanted to start questioning the women. One of them had to be the key to who killed Landers. He knew it wasn't Shandra; his gut told him someone was framing her. That someone in his mind was Doring. But Doring would be framing her after the fact. How did he get his hands on the weapon? It had to be Ms. Vincent who gave him the weapon. There wasn't anyone else who would have known Landers had a gun.

He started with the first woman after Shandra to have a restraining order against Landers.

"Hello, Ms. Parker?"

"Yes and no. I'm married. I'm Mrs. Welch now. Who are you?" The voice was quiet and meek.

"I'm Detective Ryan Greer with the Weippe County Sheriff's Office in Idaho."

"Oh! Why are you contacting me? I haven't done anything. And my husband is a good man."

"Ma'am, I just have some questions to ask you about a restraining order you had on Carl Landers."

The line went silent, not a breath or noise. "Mrs. Welch. I'm not trying to drag up bad memories. But Landers has been killed and the current suspect was also a victim of his."

"My husband doesn't know about that. I went through years of therapy to erase what that man did to me." Her voice was barely above a whisper.

"Mrs. Welch. Did you approach Dana Benham for the restraining order?"

"Yes, after the police told me to contact the women's center. She was an angel from God. She helped me get away, kept Carl away, and helped me get into therapy."

"I see. And have you been contacted by anyone claiming there are tapes of you and Landers?"

A sob on the other end of the line made him feel about an inch tall. "Mrs. Welch. If you haven't been contacted, then it's safe to say there weren't any tapes."

"I hope that's true. I don't think my marriage would stand that kind of scandal."

"I'm sorry if I ruined your day. I'm trying to keep someone who is innocent out of jail." He pushed the off button and ran a hand through his hair. He hated upsetting these women by bringing up their past lives and dredging up bad memories. But he had to in order to protect Shandra.

He heard Sheba barking and went to the front window. Shandra and the big, tri-colored mutt were having a snowball fight of sorts. Shandra tossed snowballs at the dog. She rose up on her hind legs catching or not catching the snow. The sight lightened his heart. He had to keep making these calls. He had to find the real killer.

Ryan sat back down and dialed the next number. The conversation went much the same as the first conversation.

He dialed the third number on his list. "Ms. Cantwell, I'm Ryan Greer, a detective with the Weippe County Sheriff's Office in Idaho."

"What are you calling me for?" The woman had a definite chip on her shoulder.

"I'm investigating the murder of Carl Landers."

Laughter came from the other side of the phone. "Karma's a bitch," she said. "Tell whoever did it they did the world a favor."

"I'm calling you because you were one of the women who placed a restraining order on Landers. Who did you contact to do that?"

"What's that have to do with his murder?" Her tone was belligerent.

"A suspect was one of Landers' victims. I'm trying to establish there were other people who he'd harmed." Ryan didn't like how that came out. She'd probably hang up on him.

"I knew there were others. That's why Dana contacted me. She'd helped other women get away from Carl."

"So Ms. Benham contacted you? When and why?" he asked, scribbling on a note pad.

"She saw how Carl treated me at a gallery showing and contacted me. I told her all the crap he did, and she suggested I get away from him."

"So she was keeping an eye on Landers?" he asked.

"I don't know about that, but she was right about his exploiting me. I had some woman call me six months ago saying she'd give sex tapes to my parents if I didn't give her money." Ms. Cantwell laughed. "I haven't had a good enough job to pay anyone anything after rent, utilities, and food. I told her she could do what she wanted with the tapes. No one was going to care." Another laugh. "She didn't like that and threatened to send them to the local television station. I told her go ahead. I'd tell the world what a creep Professor Carl Landers was. She hung up."

Ryan jotted down everything the woman had to say. "You didn't happen to catch the number she called from?"

"I told you, I can barely pay my rent, I don't have one of those fancy cell phones. I have a landline."

"Thank you for your time." He pushed the off button. It sounded like the blackmailer was new to the racket. A true blackmailer would have known Ms. Cantwell didn't have any money before they approached her. But her comments gave him the needed boost to call the next woman on the list.

"Hello, Ms. Chase? I'm Ryan Greer, a detective with the Weippe County Sheriff's Office in Idaho."

"Idaho? Why are you calling me?" The voice had a note of authority to it.

"I'm working on a case that involves the death of Carl Landers."

A sharp intake of breath and the sound of someone sitting down hard came across the phone.

"He's really dead?" her voice whispered.

"Yes. A woman he victimized is being wrongfully accused of his death. I'm calling others who had restraining orders against him and trying to see who else might have been harmed by him." Ryan didn't like the way his comment sounded as if she were a suspect, but he didn't know how else to phrase it.

"I didn't kill him!"

"Ma'am, I'm not accusing you. I'm trying to discover as much information as possible about his past to try and piece together who did." He tapped the pen against his notepad. "Did you contact Dana Benham?"

"No. She spotted Carl and I at a university event and approached me in the women's restroom. She said she'd helped others get away from him and offered her services for free. I jumped. When he first started dating me, he was sweet and considerate. The moment I moved into his house, he became possessive and abusive. Threatening to kill me if I left." Her voice became stronger as she talked. Ms. Chase was a lot like Shandra.

"I have another question. Were you contacted about video tapes?"

"Yes! I couldn't believe the nerve of that woman! She said for five thousand dollars she'd send me the tape and no one would ever know that it had been made. I was furious. I wanted proof she even had tapes because I never saw a camera in Carl's bedroom. She sent me a still photo of me and… It brought back so many bad memories."

"Did you pay or take it to the police?" Ryan needed to get his hands on the envelope and photo.

"My fiancé and I discussed whether or not a tape made of me by an abusive lover would cause a problem with my career. We decided it wouldn't, and I refused to pay the money. I'd told my fiancé all about Carl. He wanted to press charges. I convinced him I just wanted it in the past."

"Do you still have the envelope and photo?" Ryan sat up straighter and poised his pen over his notebook. This could be the evidence that proved someone else had reason to kill Landers.

There was a moment of silence. "I should have burned it, but I wanted to have it in case the tapes did turn up. You know to take to the police and tell them I was being blackmailed."

"Would you mind sending it overnight mail to me? I can have them dusted for fingerprints. This person sounds like an amateur. I'm hoping they didn't think about wearing gloves while handling the photo and envelope."

"I'd prefer no one be able to find out about this in court records. I'll send them to you. Where should I mail them?"

Ryan had to think about this. He wasn't on the case and shouldn't be collecting evidence. But no one else cared to look beyond Shandra. He gave her the Huckleberry Police Station. "Make sure you put on it for Detective Ryan Greer. No one else will know what they are for and you don't want others seeing them."

"I will. I'm guessing Carl was murdered if you are investigating his death. From what Dana said, I have a feeling you have a long line of suspects."

"I do. Thank you for your time and sending me the photo. I'll make sure the envelope goes to one lab tech and the photo to another. That way they can't connect you with the photo."

"Thank you. Good-bye, Detective."

The phone went silent. Ryan circled her name.

She'd asked too many questions to be a suspect and was too willing to help. He had two more names on his list. But he was beginning to wonder if the attorney Dana Benham had decided that Carl Landers was getting to old to exploit women and found a way to stop him for good.

Chapter Sixteen

Shandra spent the whole day in the studio. Knowing Ryan was handling finding answers, she concentrated on her latest vase. She'd named it "Free Spirit". That was how she felt knowing once they found Carl's killer she would be free of her past forever.

The dream from the night before and the vision of Grandmother slipped in and out of her mind as she worked. Whose family was Ella talking about? Mine and how they would have comforted me if I had only turned to them? Or the women who Carl terrorized, or Carl's family?

He had taken her to three family gatherings while she was with him. All were within the first year, before she'd started losing weight and he'd only verbally abused her at home, not in public. His mother had been forceful and domineering. Traits Carl had inherited. She'd noticed a rapier tongue on the woman but had put it off as old age and how some people as they grew older tended to be nastier. Alexis, Carl's sister, had been aloof, ignoring her brother and smothering her mother, begging for attention. Carl had told Shandra, Alexis was jealous of him and his relationship with his mother.

And I'd thought my family was dysfunctional before attending the Landers' family gatherings.

Shandra shook those thoughts off and moved to Sidney framing her. That she understood. The man had a mean streak and vengefulness. But did he kill Carl or did someone else?

The front door to the studio opened.

"Are you going to work all day and all night?" Ryan asked.

She glanced up and smiled. "Things were going so well, I forgot the time." She set down the knife she used to make cutouts in the vase and tossed a light-weight cloth over the creation.

"You don't want me to see what you're making?" he asked, walking over to the pottery wheel.

"I may change my mind. I don't like anyone to see what I'm doing until it's ready to fire." Shandra stood, stretched her hands over her head, and bent backwards. "I didn't feel like I'd been sitting there that long but now that I've stood…"

"I can massage those knots out of your back," Ryan offered, stepping closer and kneading her shoulder muscles.

"That's good." She closed her eyes and centered her mind on relaxing her muscles.

"I made chili, and I have some news." He spoke quietly in her ear, his warm breath puffing against her neck.

"Good news?" She opened her eyes and spun to

face him.

"Good news for us until we can figure out how to get it to Pete and Stu without them thinking we're stacking evidence to keep them from looking at you." He shrugged.

"I'll take whatever we can get." She linked her arm through his. "I'm starving."

"I brought you a sandwich at noon."

"It was delicious, but it's worn off." As if to punctuate her statement, her stomach growled.

Ryan laughed. "Good thing I made a big pot of chili and cornbread."

"I like a man who can cook." She patted her leg.

Sheba crawled out from under the table, loping out the door ahead of them. She bounded into the trees, disappearing among the brush and snow.

"I guess she doesn't want dinner," Ryan said.

"She only went out once today."

They entered the kitchen door. Savory smells of corn bread and spicy chili assaulted her nose and started her mouth watering.

"If it tastes as good as it smells, you may cook any time." She shed her coat and boots, moving into the laundry room to wash up.

Ryan continued to the kitchen.

Shandra watched the water pooling in the sink turn the yellow brown color of the clay she'd worked with all day and wondered if it was the same kind found on the cloth with the weapon that killed Carl. If it was, someone had entered her studio without anyone seeing and stole the rag. A shiver slid down her back. She'd always felt safe hidden away on the mountain. Knowing someone had been here and taken something from her studio, made her feel vulnerable.

"It's time to put a lock on all the buildings."

"What?" Ryan asked, sticking his head in the laundry room.

"I'm thinking with someone possibly walking into my studio and taking a rag, I need to make sure the studio and the barn have locks on them. And that Lil and I lock them when we aren't in there."

Ryan pulled her out of the laundry room. "I don't think you need to get that drastic. I do agree they need to be locked at night and when you're gone. You don't know that Doring or whoever took that rag didn't come in here when you were on a trip and Lil went to town."

"Or at night while we were sleeping." Shandra stared into his eyes. She loved that he believed in her. But he couldn't sugar-coat everything.

They dished up food and sat at the counter before Ryan pulled his notebook from his laptop and flipped it open.

"The first two women I contacted weren't blackmailed. The next one was, but had no money and laughed at the person. Which leads me to believe it was an amateur. Someone who came across the tapes and thought they'd make some money."

"Woman or man?" she asked between bites of chili.

"Woman."

She put her spoon down and stared at him. "Please tell me it wasn't nice Mrs. Martinez?"

"It wasn't. The three that were blackmailed said the voice sounded like a young woman, no accent." Ryan buttered a piece of cornbread.

"Young woman. One of Carl's latest conquests?"

she asked.

"Or Ms. Vincent." He bit into the cornbread.

"That would make sense. She finds the tapes, thinks she'll make some extra money…" A thought struck her. "How does she prove to the women she has tapes on them?"

Ryan smiled, held up a finger, and took a drink of his iced tea. "She sent a photo of the woman and Carl in a compromising position. Two of the women are sending the envelope and photo to me at the Huckleberry Station. I'm hoping we can get some prints off of them. I promised no one would know where it came from or who is in the photo."

"Did they pay?" Shandra's heart went out to the women. First to be hurt by Carl and then blackmailed.

"One didn't. She and her fiancé felt it wasn't tragic enough to hurt her career and refused to pay the five thousand the blackmailer requested." Ryan spooned chili into his mouth and chewed.

"But others did pay the money?"

"Two. They are sending me the letters they received and the directions of how to deposit the money." He flipped a couple of pages on his notepad. "They were both given the same deposit number at the same bank."

She stared at Ryan. "Really? This is an amateur. If either of those people had gone to the police, the blackmailer would be behind bars right now."

He grinned. "I gave the information to a friend in the Albuquerque police."

"Albuquerque? As in Tabby?" Shandra couldn't believe it was that easy. "If she was blackmailing, maybe Carl found out and she killed him. We know she had access to the weapon if it was really Carl's." She stopped the spoon halfway to her mouth. "Have you learned anything about the weapon?"

"I phoned Cathleen at home. She said it was a twenty-two derringer and the bullet that killed Landers was from the pistol that was found with the rag that incriminates you. The weapon was registered to Carl Landers. So now it isn't premeditated murder which kind of blows the theory you were lying in wait for him to come to the mountain. Unless they find records of him calling you."

"You were with me the whole time. He never called. I don't think my phone even rang after I returned."

"But you could have scheduled to meet when you were in New Mexico."

She narrowed her eyes. "I thought you believed me?"

"I do, but that's what Pete could say. Especially with Ms. Vincent saying Landers came here to see you."

Shandra growled and crumbled a piece of cornbread in her chili. "That woman lies more than she spouts the truth. She has to be behind the blackmail and the killing."

Chapter Seventeen

Shandra and Ryan had spent a quiet Sunday making a list of the things they knew and circles for the unknowns. After they were both tired of thinking about it, they went snowshoeing through the forest. They'd trudged for three hours to get to her fence line. The ski runs were another twenty miles away. The idea she and Sheba could have walked to the ski runs to meet Carl was ludicrous. It would have taken her a day to get there and one to get back by snowshoe.

While cleaning up the breakfast dishes Monday morning, Shandra looked back at the previous day and smiled. She enjoyed spending leisurely time with Ryan. This morning she was headed to the studio to work on the new project. She started out the back door when Sheba's greeting bark erupted at the front of the house. Ryan had headed down the mountain to see if any of the blackmail evidence had arrived at the Huckleberry Police Station.

She stepped out of her boots and hung her coat and

hat back up before heading to the front door. She glanced out the front window and her heart lodged in her throat. The two State Police Detectives stood in front of their vehicle eyeballing Sheba, who crouched down, waiting for the men to play with her.

Her first thought was to leave them standing there. Sheba wouldn't hurt a fly, and she could sneak out into the forest and wait for them to leave. But that was the coward's way out and she had nothing to hide.

She took a deep breath and pulled the door open. "Good morning! Sheba. Come."

Sheba bounced up, trotted to Shandra, and through the door.

The two men followed a few yards behind.

When they were all inside, Shandra faced the detectives. "Do you want to sit in the main room or in the kitchen while I make coffee?"

Pete nodded to the kitchen.

She led the way and went straight to the coffee maker, filling it with water and the right amount of grounds. "You missed Ryan. He left about an hour ago," she said by way of small talk.

"We know. When we saw him enter town, we headed this way," Stu said.

Shandra spun around. "Why would you wait to get me alone? I don't like this." She walked to the back door.

"Where are you going?" Pete lunged at her and grabbed her arm.

She glared at him and shook his hold loose. "I'm calling Lil in so you don't put words in my mouth." She opened the door and grabbed the metal bar to the dinner bell that hung by the back door. Shandra rattled the bar around the triangle shape until she spotted Lil carrying her walking stick and hurrying her way.

"Take your time, but do come in!" she called and closed the door.

Back in the kitchen, she said, "I have nothing to hide, but I'll be damned if I'll have you railroad me by twisting my words."

Pete stared at the folder in front of him, and Stu glared back at her.

Lil burst through the door, spotted the two men, and her face turned into a stony frown as she raised her walking stick in a threatening pose. "I knew somethin' was up the way you were whanging on that bell."

"Lil, hang up your things and join us for coffee. Since they waited until Ryan left to come talk to me, I thought it would be good to have another person present." Shandra set cups in front of the two detectives and a spot at the end of the counter for Lil.

And to be even safer, Shandra fiddled with her cell phone, found the record app and pressed it while her back was to her guests. She left the phone sitting on the counter as she placed cream and sugar out and poured the coffee.

She took a stool on the opposite end of the counter from Lil, leaving the detectives sitting on the side. "What did you come here to ask?"

"It seems tapes were brought to the attention of the Albuquerque Police that came from Carl Landers' home," Pete said, watching her.

"Really?" She didn't want to get Ryan in trouble by saying anything about the investigating he'd been doing on her behalf.

"Were they of Carl and women?" she asked.

Stu narrowed his eyes. "Why would you ask that?"

"I can only guess considering what the woman with Sidney Doring said to me the other day in the diner." She wanted to ask if they knew people were blackmailed over those tapes but that would tell them she knew too much.

"Aren't you going to ask if you are on them?"

Shandra's cheeks heated. "I hope I'm not and quite frankly if I am, I'd rather not know. That was a time in my life when I'd become Carl's puppet."

Lil gasped. "Shandra what are you talking about?"

She peered down the counter to her employee and friend. "I'll tell you about it later."

The empathy in the older woman's eyes made her even more grateful Lil had been belligerent about leaving the ranch when she bought the place.

Pete looked back and forth between her and Lil like a person watching a tennis match. "There were no tapes of you. He must have started taping his lovers after that." Pete opened the folder in front of him. "We found the weapon. It was under a tree between your property and the ski run."

Shandra shook her head. "I told you. I wasn't anywhere near that ski run. I hadn't been more than a hundred yards from my house since I returned from New Mexico."

"I can vouch for that. She never left the place until Wednesday morning when she went to town to have lunch with Ryan." Lil nodded her spiked head like a flail of a knight riding into battle.

"How do you account for the fact a rag with potter's clay was wrapped around the pistol?" Pete asked, opening the folder and placing a photo in front of her.

Shandra stared at the photo. "Your killer is someone from New Mexico."

Pete narrowed his eyes. "What are you talking about?"

She put a finger on the rag. "This rag is one I used at the workshop I taught at the university. It's an industrial rag. The sides are hemmed. The kind I use here are true rags. I buy them by the box from the Warner Humane Society Thrift Store. They are cut from clothing that is donated and too stained or worn out to sell. I have a box of them in my studio I can show you."

She slid the photo down the counter to Lil.

"Yep. That's not one of the rags Shandra uses here." Lil stabbed a finger at the photo. "And that's not the color of her clay."

"That's clay bought from a manufacturer. I dig clay from the mountain and purify it myself. It has an earthier tint to it." Shandra stood. "Come out to the studio, I'll show you." She walked to the door, pulled on her coat, and stepped into her boots.

The second she pulled on the door, Sheba came bounding down the hallway. Shandra hid a snicker as the two men flattened against the wall. Lil didn't hide her chuckle.

The men followed her out to the studio.

Knowing the rag came from New Mexico and not from her studio, made her breathe easier. That meant no one had trespassed into her space.

At the studio, Sheba trotted over to her bed under the glazing table and lay down.

Shandra picked up the box of rags in the corner.

"Here. And in the wastebasket you can see used ones." She toed the metal industrial receptacle sitting beside the rag box. A varied array of colored rags with yellowish brown dried clay on them filled the bottom third of the container.

She turned to the men. "It makes no sense I would bring a rag from my workshop in New Mexico and wrap it around a murder weapon here. That would be stupid. Your killer has to be someone who picked that up after the workshop and brought it with them to incriminate me." She waved her hand from the rags to the waste basket. "Someone who had never set foot in my studio or seen my work in the first stages."

The door burst open. "What are you two doing here?" Ryan demanded.

Stu spun toward the door, while Pete kept his gaze on her.

Shandra crossed the studio and stood by Ryan. "They brought me a photo of the rag." She smiled at him. "It's not one of mine. It is one I used at the workshop in New Mexico."

He put an arm around her waist and glared at the detectives. "More proof Shandra is being set up."

Pete shook his head. "Just because she says the rag comes from somewhere else doesn't mean she didn't do it."

Shandra shoved her hands on her hips. "Why are you so ready to pin this on me? I didn't kill him. Someone is trying to make it look like me."

Stu smirked. "We get that a lot."

"I understand videos taken by Landers have surfaced." Ryan narrowed his eyes and studied the two men. He'd thought having Pete on the case would give

Shandra a fair deal, but now he wasn't so sure. When he'd arrived at the Huckleberry Police Station, Hazel told him that the two State Detectives were waiting for him to come to town alone. He'd gathered the overnight envelopes waiting for him and headed straight back to Shandra's.

"How do you know?" Stu asked. "You aren't a part of this investigation."

"I have my sources. I may not be able to work the case, but I have access to information." When he'd seen the State SUV as he drove up, he'd slid the blackmail letters that were sent to him under the seat of his truck. Finding the house empty, he'd hurried to the studio. There was a reason the two had wanted Shandra alone.

Ryan grabbed Shandra's hand. "Was Shandra in any of the videos?"

Pete glanced to their clasped hands and shook his head. "No. We're running down the others. Only their first names were on the tapes."

He squeezed her hand. They were a step ahead of the investigation thanks to his having looked up the restraining orders and connecting the last name with the names Aldo found on the tapes. But he'd have to hand over the blackmail information as soon as he and Shandra looked it over.

Ryan opened the door and motioned with his free hand. "Good luck finding them. I hope when you do, you realize there are a lot more people who would have liked to see Landers dead than Shandra."

Pete walked to the door and stopped in front of him. "You're a good cop. Don't risk your career." He glanced at Shandra and back to Ryan.

"Shandra didn't kill Landers. I'm betting my career

and my future on it."

The two men left and Ryan closed the door. He pulled Shandra into an embrace. There was no way the woman in his arms killed Landers. And he'd prove it.

Chapter Eighteen

Shandra picked up the cups in the kitchen and put the kettle on for tea. Her churning stomach couldn't take any more coffee today.

Ryan walked in the back door. He'd gone to his pickup to retrieve the information sent to him from the blackmail victims.

"Here or in the main room?" she asked, holding a tray laden with tea pot, cups, and cookies.

"Main room." He hung up his coat and slipped out of his boots.

She set the tray on the coffee table and settled onto the couch with her legs drawn up under her.

Ryan pulled out the knife hanging on his belt, slit open all three envelopes, and sat beside her.

"We're lucky they trusted you enough to send you this information." She'd thought about it last night drifting off to sleep. Perhaps knowing the man behind the videos was dead the women felt free just as she did.

Without touching the contents of the envelopes, he dumped them out on the coffee table. A letter and a photo slid out of each packet. Two of them had an additional slip of paper. Ryan pulled on a pair of rubber gloves and moved the papers and photos so they could see the people and the wording on the letters.

"Same print on each letter," he said.

Shandra stared at the photos. The painting over the bed, the bed frame, the color on the walls. The room brought back flashes of the pain and humiliation she'd received there.

Ryan put an arm around her shoulders and squeezed. "You okay?"

"I thought I'd put it all behind. But seeing the room…"

"I won't let anyone hurt you again. And Landers can't hurt you anymore." He kissed her temple. "If the photos bother you, read the letters and see if you can glean anything from them."

Ryan moved the photos to the far side of the table and slid the letters to the side closest to them.

She reached down to put her finger on the zip code where the money was to be sent.

He grabbed her hand, keeping her from touching the letter.

"That zip code is the one used by the abuse center where Dana Benham worked." She didn't want to think the woman who set her and the other women free was using their own tortured pasts to make money.

Ryan studied her. "You're sure?"

"Yes. She sent me several letters and I sent her a thank you card and payment afterwards." Shandra leaned back. "I hope it isn't her. She did so much good, it would be a shame for her to ruin it all by having blackmailed her clients and killed a man."

He picked up an envelope and started putting everything back in.

"Wait!" Shandra studied the photo he held and then studied the others. "From the angle of those photos he must have had the camera hidden in the closet." She hated having such a surge of relief. It seemed unfair to the women who'd followed her in Carl's life. "I know there wasn't a camera in that closet when I lived there. See the angle? That would have been up on a shelf. There was no shelf or anything up in that area of the closet. It had shelves on the sides but the rod to hang clothes was the only thing in the middle." She hugged Ryan. "There aren't any videos of me."

"I'm glad." He kissed her. "Let's get these back in an envelope, and we'll drive to Warner and hand them over to Cathleen, who can put them in evidence for Pete and Stu."

Shandra sat back while Ryan put the letters and photos into a plastic evidence bag. He stood, crossed to the gas fireplace, and tossed the envelopes with his name and the Huckleberry Police Department into the fire. He watched them burn, then came back to the couch.

"I think I should call the P.I. who found the tapes and have him do a background check on Ms. Benham." Ryan pulled out his phone, dialed, and started talking.

Shandra poured the tea, listened to his side of the conversation, and waited from him to finish. She sipped her tea and nibbled on a cookie.

Ryan finished the call and picked up a cookie. "Aldo will look into Ms. Benham."

"Are you going to get into trouble for gathering information and not letting the State detectives do their job?" She had worried about this from the beginning but after Pete mentioned it this morning it had stuck with her.

"I'll probably get demoted, a reprimand, or probation. But if we can find the killer and show you're innocence, it's worth it."

She grasped his hand. "I don't want you to jeopardize your career. I'm innocent. Pete and Stu should eventually figure that out."

"You are worth jeopardizing my career." Ryan raised her hand and kissed it.

She shook her head. "I don't know whether to be flattered you are willing to hurt your career or mortified you are risking so much."

"Be flattered." He downed the rest of his tea. "Let's clean this up and head for Warner. The sooner these are out of our hands and into the hands of people who are running the investigation, the better."

Shandra couldn't agree more.

***

Ryan not only wanted to leave the blackmail letters with Cathleen to keep his duplicity in collecting the information from being found out, he also needed more clothes from his place. On the drive to Warner, he called Cathleen and asked her to meet them at a rundown tavern that was rarely visited by law enforcement. Even though she was his sister and there shouldn't be any talk, he didn't want someone knowing he'd visited with her and then the information showed up.

Pete had been right. He had a lot on the line sticking up for Shandra and going against his forced vacation and digging into the case. He hoped his involvement would be overlooked when the real killer was brought to justice.

Shandra clung to his arm as they entered the Dark Horse Tavern. "You sure this is a good place to have lunch?" she asked.

Half a dozen bikers were playing pool. A table had an older, raggedy couple nursing beers, and two men in their seventies played checkers at the bar.

"Do they even serve food?" Shandra asked as Ryan settled her in a booth seat.

He grinned and pulled a grungy looking menu from behind the napkin holder. Ryan studied the menu. "It looks like you can have a hamburger and jo-jos or chicken strips and jo-jos."

"No salad or soup?" Shandra asked.

"Nope."

The bald-headed man that stood behind the bar when they walked in, ambled over. "Ain't seen you two before."

"Passing through and meeting a friend." Ryan nodded to Shandra. "Burger or Chicken?"

"Burger please and an iced tea," she said.

"I'll have the same." He put the menu back behind the napkin holder.

The bartender trudged back to the kitchen with their order.

Ryan leaned close to Shandra. "We're safe. No one or anything is going to hurt us."

"You'd think I'd be comfortable in a place like this, but I'm not."

"Why would you be comfortable?" He studied Shandra.

"I was on the rodeo circuit for a year before my

stepfather figured out my heart wasn't in competing." She shrugged. "But the people were nice. After the rodeos everyone would go to a western bar or a run-down place like this and party."

Ryan picked up her hand. "You partied?"

She shook her head. "No. I don't like to drink and be out of control. But I'd go along and usually drive the drunk cowboys back to the rodeo grounds where they'd crash in campers and tents until the next go-round the following day."

"You've lived a diverse life." Ryan had known from the moment he met Shandra, she had a unique story. The more he heard, the more he came to admire about her.

The door opened. The bright sunshine reflected off the snow outside making it hard to see if a man or woman walked in. The door shut, and his eyes adjusted to the dimness.

Cathleen stood just inside the door. Ryan figured she was allowing her eyes to adjust to the dimness of the establishment. She spotted them and strode their way, taking the bench seat across the table from him and Shandra.

"I know you're on an unofficial vacation but why couldn't we meet at the deli or the Shake Shack?" Cathleen asked, slipping out of her coat. Her deputy sheriff's uniform seemed to glow in the light of the single watt bulb hanging over the booth.

The bartender arrived with the iced teas and eyed Cathleen. "What'll you have?"

"They only have burgers and chicken strips with jo-jos," Shandra said.

"Tea like them, and I'll have the chicken strips, no

jo-jos." Cathleen set her coat over on the booth next to the wall and watched the bartender walk away. "I repeat. Why did you pick this place?"

Ryan knew his sister would do anything for him but what he was asking could jeopardize her career. "We have evidence that needs to come to the attention of the detectives working the case."

"But you don't want them to know you dug it up?" Cathleen shook her head. "This could cost you your job."

"I told him things will work out. He doesn't need to risk his career," Shandra said, siding with his sister.

He clasped Shandra's hand and stared into his sister's eyes. "I won't have them hanging her without digging farther. All the evidence they have so far is circumstantial."

"That's why she hasn't been read her rights. Ryan, you've worked with these men before. They aren't going to arrest her unless they have solid proof. And they aren't going to find any." Cathleen stared into Shandra's eyes. "Right?"

"I didn't kill Carl. I didn't even know he was in Huckleberry until he was dead." Shandra stirred her iced tea with the straw, but her gaze remained on the woman sitting across from her.

"I believe you. What is the evidence you have?" Cathleen asked, then leaned back as the bartender approached.

He set an iced tea in front of her and baskets with burgers in front of Shandra and Ryan.

"Yours will be out in three minutes." The bartender pivoted on one foot and strode across the room.

"I don't know how much you know about Landers

and Shandra's past…"

"Not much. They knew each other." Cathleen's gaze flit back and forth between them.

"I don't want to go into all the details, but he abused me, and I used a restraining order to get away from him." Shandra picked up a jo-jo and dunked it in a container of pink sauce in her basket.

"I see. Is this why they think you killed Landers? Well, that, and the evidence they keep finding." Cathleen stirred her drink.

Ryan's heart raced. "Have they found something besides the gun and rag?"

"No." Cathleen sipped her tea.

"I refuted those this morning." Shandra bit into a jo-jo.

The woman leaned across the table. "How?"

"I showed the detectives the rag that was with the weapon was from the workshop I did in New Mexico. It was an industrial rag, one the university provided for me. And the clay on it is one the university purchased for me to use during the workshop. It has a different color than the clay I purify from the mountain. Someone from New Mexico brought that rag here to frame me."

"We keep finding proof, but Pete doesn't believe us." Ryan smeared a jo-jo around in ketchup.

Cathleen stared at him. "They're only doing the same thing you would if you were on the case."

"They aren't as open-minded." He put a hand on Shandra's knee and squeezed. Looking at those photos had been hard on her. He couldn't imagine what she'd went through at the hands of Landers. "Did they believe you about the rag and clay?" he asked.

"I think so. I'm sure they'll contact the university and check on what I said. Anyone could have plucked that rag out of the waste basket or dumpster." She picked up the burger. "We just have to keep finding proof for all their accusations." She took a big bite and chewed.

The bartender returned with Cathleen's chicken strips.

"Thank you," she said.

The bartender grunted, put the ticket on the table, and left.

"This food isn't that bad." Shandra dunked another jo-jo in sauce.

Cathleen picked at her chicken strips. "Are you going to tell me what evidence you're handing me?"

"Other women were abused by Landers. He filmed them in bed with him. We discovered three who were blackmailed. They sent me the photos and letter from the blackmailer. Only two paid but then never received the tape. They would be my first guess at having killed Landers, but they both live in California and it seems too elaborate to try and implicate Shandra when chances are they don't even know about her." Ryan bit into his burger. Shandra was right. It wasn't half bad. He chewed and studied his sister.

"But you have someone you believe might be the murderer?" Cathleen broke a strip of chicken in half. Steam rose in front of her face.

"Two actually," Shandra said.

"Two?"

"We're working on narrowing it down. Tabitha Vincent, the woman who came to Idaho with Landers, and an attorney who works for a women's abuse center in Albuquerque." He sipped his tea. They still had a lot of digging to do.

Cathleen picked up another chicken strip and waved it around like a conductor's baton. "The evidence you're giving me is against one of these women?"

"We hope once they are dusted for prints there will be the same set on each one and it will be one of the two women we suspect." Ryan shrugged and took another bite of his burger.

Chapter Nineteen

Shandra snuggled under the blanket on the couch reading up on a technique she wanted to apply to her "Free Spirit" vase. Sheba snored by the fire, and Ryan had his nose in his computer. He'd been engrossed for over an hour.

"What are you looking up?" she finally asked.

"Court records for cases Ms. Benham took to court. She has an unusually high number of pro-bono abuse cases. But her financial records show she is barely paying her bills."

"You think she tried to blackmail her clients? Isn't that unethical besides being illegal?" She thought about the woman who'd helped her nine years ago. "Dana doesn't strike me as the type to use others sorrow to make money for herself. She worked long hours. When I talked with her, all she asked of me were the court costs. I sent her more later, after I left New Mexico."

"Did you send it from Huckleberry?" Ryan's eyes focused on her.

"No. It was when I was living with a friend in Montana." Shandra flipped the magazine closed. "I think we need to focus on Tabby. She is the most likely to have blackmailed, had access to the rag and the pistol, and may have the best reason."

"What reason would that be?" he asked, closing the computer.

"She isn't Carl's typical "victim". I wonder if they didn't have some kind of a partnership. She didn't act like a grieving lover at the diner or at the lodge."

"I have the P.I. looking into her as well." Ryan leaned close. "I'm headed to bed." He kissed her on the lips, lingered, then drew back and stood.

"Goodnight. Sheba and I will be heading to bed in a few minutes." Shandra opened the magazine back up.

"I'll lock the back door." Ryan disappeared down the hall.

She watched his back. Once this was over, she wanted to forget about the past and try for a future with Ryan. Closing the magazine, she rose, turned off the lights, and entered her bedroom.

Sheba crawled up on the bed and took her spot at the foot, all sprawled out, tail at one side and her muzzle hanging over the other.

She climbed into bed, wondering how they'd fit Ryan in this bed when she was ready. Sheba wouldn't like being ousted.

***

Shandra ran down the snow-covered mountain. Her heart pumped. Someone was chasing her. She felt the need to hide. A large pine tree stood to the left. She veered that direction, knowing the person could follow her tracks, but she wanted to be hidden rather than in the open ski run.

She ran into something as big around as a tree trunk but felt like cloth. She looked up a long leg. Hands held the contraptions that make marionettes move. She couldn't see the face but blonde hair blew in the breeze. A woman.

Before Shandra could move, Tabby came into view. She smiled as her hand raised. Her red fingernails gave a wicked aura to the revolver in her hand. A revolver that looked like Ryan's Glock.

"What have you done to Ryan?" Shandra asked, backing into the leg.

"I took care of a problem."

"No!"

A heavy weight pressed down on Shandra and something wide and wet swiped the side of her face. She pushed at the weight and encounter the long, fluffy fur of Sheba.

She wrapped her arms around Sheba and stared into the darkness. "We have to prove Tabby killed Carl." And who was the woman using Tabby like a puppet? Hugging Sheba, she finally fell asleep.

***

Shandra slept fitfully the rest of the night and woke early. Ryan wasn't up yet, so she set to work making cinnamon rolls. She needed something to occupy her mind and her hands until she could tell him about the dream.

The rolls were rising when he shuffled down the hall. He'd dressed in a faded flannel shirt and jeans. Since his forced vacation, she'd been seeing more of the real Ryan as he stayed with her. She liked what she saw.

"I take it you're not planning to go anywhere today?" she asked, pouring a cup of coffee and placing it on the counter in front of him.

"No. I can get all the information I need right here from my computer." He smiled. "The smells and scenery in here are too good to leave."

Shandra smiled and let herself enjoy being flattered. Since Carl, she'd shied away from men who teased and flattered. She didn't want to get caught in something she couldn't get out of. Ryan was proving once again he cared for her and wanted the best for her.

"Cinnamon rolls will be ready in thirty minutes." She hooked her coffee cup from beside the sink and sat down next to Ryan. "I had a dream last night."

He swiveled on the stool, giving her his complete attention.

She still marveled at how when they'd first met he'd believed in her dreams before she did. He'd encouraged her to believe in them too, that she had a gift. One that few people would understand and most would laugh at.

"What did you dream about?" He picked up his cup and sipped as he scanned her face.

"I was running down the ski slope trying to get away from someone. I ran to hide behind a tree and smacked into something as large as a tree but wasn't." She studied Ryan. This dream made her believe there was more than one person involved in Carl's death. But the symbolism caused her to wonder at her understanding of the dream.

"Why wasn't it a tree?"

"It was cloth. I looked up and it was a person, a woman's leg. She was tall, taller than the trees, had blonde hair and was holding those wood things that move puppets." Shandra took a sip of her coffee to settle her mind.

"Could you tell who she was?" he asked, putting a hand on her knee.

"No. Then Tabby ran around the tree and pointed your revolver at me. She said you were…" She couldn't say it. "I screamed and then woke up to Sheba licking me and covering me with her body."

Ryan put his cup down and wrapped his arms around her. "I won't let anything happen to me. We have to find out who is pulling Ms. Vincent's strings." He squeezed her and kissed her temple. "Are you going to be okay?"

"Yeah. These dreams. They feel so real." She peered into his eyes and saw empathy.

"That's why I believe in them." He kissed her lips and released her.

Ryan picked up his coffee and headed into the main room. "I'll go see if Aldo sent me any information while I wait for the cinnamon rolls."

**

After breakfast, Ryan led Shandra into the main room. "Aldo sent me several reports. I want you to read them."

She opened the first report. It detailed Tabby's life in and out of court. The name of the person who attended the hearings with Tabby was Dana Benham.

"I can't believe Dana—"

Sheba barked a welcome.

Ryan rose and looked out the window. "It's Pete and Stu."

"Again?" She'd had enough of the two and didn't

want to talk to them today. She shut the laptop and set it on the coffee table. Pulling her legs up underneath her, she tugged on a print blanket to cover her cold body and waited as Ryan let the two into the house.

Ryan greeted the staters more congenially than he felt. He also didn't miss the way Pete scanned his faded shirt and jeans, and slippers. Yes, he was making himself at home at Shandra's. He didn't plan on leaving here until they'd found the killer and cleared her.

"You're out and about early," he said, closing the door behind them and waving them into the main room where Shandra had curled up under a blanket. Sheba sat beside her, watching the two newcomers.

"We were given evidence of women from Carl Landers' past who were being blackmailed," Pete said, sitting on one of the chairs across the coffee table from the couch.

Ryan sat on the couch beside Shandra. Stu sat on the chair an end table away from Pete.

"You wouldn't know anything about this would you?" Pete asked, pulling the envelope with the letters and envelopes out of a folder and placing it on the coffee table.

"With the woman who came here with Landers trying to rile Shandra up with talk of tapes, we hired a private investigator to look into the allegations."

"The same one who told the Albuquerque police about the tapes?" Stu asked.

Ryan nodded. "I called up the women and talked with them. The blackmailer was an amateur. The only people besides Landers to have access to the videos to get the stills and blackmail were the housekeeper and the woman living with him. The housekeeper checks out as not the blackmailer. That leaves one other person. Tabitha Vincent." He didn't stop there. "She had access to the weapon, was in Albuquerque when Shandra gave her workshop and could have picked up the rag, and she has a rap sheet that goes back to her teens."

"We know all of this. But she has an alibi." Pete said.

Ryan shook his head. "No, she doesn't."

Pete nodded. "She was with Sydney Doring all night."

Shandra leaned forward. "That man would lie to his mother if it got him money or a woman."

"She wasn't with Doring. The morning we found the body, before I was pulled off the case, both Doring and Ms. Vincent said they were alone all night." He stared at Pete. "They're both lying."

"I had your notes and asked them about it. They said they didn't want you to think badly of them for hooking up so soon."

Pete's sour expression mirrored Ryan's gut. The two were chronic liars and as sleazy as it got.

"We also made a connection between the women who were blackmailed and a lawyer who specializes in domestic abuse cases." Ryan threw that into the mix.

"But I doubt she had anything to do with killing Carl," Shandra added.

Pete zeroed in on Shandra. "Why's that?"

"Because she was dedicated to helping women get out of bad situations. I can't see where she would have gained anything by killing Carl."

"Unless he found out she was using his tapes for blackmail," Ryan said.

"I don't think she did it. Tabby, yes. Dana, no." Shandra crossed her arms and stared at him.

He smiled. She was pretty sure it wasn't the lawyer. He'd go with her gut instinct any day. That and her dreams.

"I think you need to do more investigating into the blackmail and see if it points to Ms. Vincent." Ryan said, making a motion of standing.

Pete gestured for him to sit back down. "There's the little matter of you investigating this while you're supposed to be on administrative leave."

"There is no law against hiring a private investigator to look up information on people." Ryan waved his hand over the laptop. "You can learn all you need on the internet these days."

"You know what I'm talking about. If you continue investigating, I'll slap you with unpaid administrative leave and obstruction of justice."

Anger flashed through him. "How can it be obstruction of justice when I'm finding information that can lead to a killer? I'm not keeping any information we find from you."

Pete's gaze slid to Shandra and back to Ryan. "Because you are living with a person of interest in this case."

"I won't leave her here to be railroaded by you." Ryan stood. "I know the law and I know when a boundary might be crossed. So far, all we've done is expedite your discovery of information about the case. We have done nothing to keep you from investigating or giving you false evidence, which is more than I can say for Ms. Vincent and Sydney Doring." He turned to Stu. "Did you two know the brother of a woman who was abused by Landers is part of the band at the Lodge bar? He has more reason than anyone to kill Landers. His sister committed suicide because of the blackmail call she received."

He could tell by the glances between the two detectives they hadn't uncovered Woody York.

"He seems like a really nice person. But if I had a sister and she died because of what Carl did, then you might have a case against me," Shandra said, her eyes reflecting sympathy for Woody.

"What's this guy's name?" Pete asked, pulling out a pen and poising it above the file folder.

"Woody York. His sister was Shelly. I don't think he did it, but you never know. Some grief is harder to bear than others." Ryan walked to the door and waited. He knew they had only just received the blackmail information, however if he had been on the case, he would have dug through there and checked out the women before running here and complaining he'd handed them more evidence in a case.

Once the detectives left, he refilled their cups and sat on the couch beside Shandra. "We need to dig more into Ms. Vincent. If she didn't pull the trigger, she knows who did."

"I agree. For Sidney and Tabby to tell you they were alone, then tell the State detectives they were together… they are both hiding something. Whether it's shooting Carl or it's something else, they are lying."

Chapter Twenty

Ryan held the pickup door for Shandra and escorted her up the walkway to the lodge. After the detectives left, he'd dug up a bit more on Tabby. That information had Shandra wanting to question the staff at the lodge.

"Do you think the detectives will be here?" she asked.

Ryan held the door open and shrugged. "I would think if they came straight here from your place they would have left by now."

Shandra hoped so. After their comments to Ryan about him obstructing justice, she didn't want to get him in trouble because she felt she could learn something about Sidney and Tabby's whereabouts the night Carl died.

"Look it's Meredith." She scooted across the lobby and followed the woman who was the manager of the lodge. They'd worked together on a couple of art events held here.

"Meredith? Meredith?" Shandra called as she closed the distance between them.

The woman spun around. A smile spread across her face. "Shandra! What a surprise."

"Hello." Shandra stopped and held her hand out to the woman. They shook and Shandra drew Ryan forward. "Meredith Gamble, this is my friend, Ryan Greer. Ryan, Meredith."

"Pleased to meet you, Ms. Gamble." Ryan shook hands with Meredith.

"Please, call me Meredith. We aren't as formal as most businesses our size."

"Yes, that's what makes this lodge so inviting," Shandra said, meaning it and hoping it helped her grease the woman's vocal chords about the lodge and the owner, Sydney Doring.

The woman's cheeks blushed as she pushed her horn-rimmed glasses higher up her nose and smiled. "Thank you. Hosting the art events is a boon to our business in the summer months. Right now with all this snow, we don't have enough rooms to accommodate everyone who wants to stay here."

"Sydney would be in a world of hurt without you running things for him," Shandra said. She knew the woman wasn't crazy about her philandering boss.

"If he'd spend as much time looking at the books and okaying repairs and updates as he did playing room tag with the wealthy women staying here, this place could accommodate more skiers."

"I thought I saw him in the bar the other night with a young blonde woman," Shandra said.

"Ms. Vincent. I thought she'd be gone when her benefactor was found dead on the slope." Meredith huffed and showed definite dislike for Tabby.

"I'm sure the police told her not to leave town," Ryan slipped in.

Meredith tilted her head to the left as if thinking. "That could be. They've talked to her nearly every day. But she isn't paying for her room. Mr. Doring is comping it."

"Really? Why would he do that for a woman he barely knows?" Shandra had worked the three of them into an alcove off the main hallway.

"He's getting to know her, pretty well. Her and the woman in room four-twenty-seven. If he's not with one, he's with the other." Meredith shook her head and pursed her lips. "He isn't even discreet. Which will cost us several of the regulars if I can't keep them happy with perks and such."

"Is the woman in four-twenty-seven a regular?" Shandra asked.

"No. She arrived the day that poor man was found dead." Meredith tilted her head again. "But she knows Ms. Vincent."

"What is this woman's name?" Ryan asked.

"Mrs. Talridge."

"Does she have a set time she eats dinner in the restaurant?" Shandra asked, wanting a look at this woman.

"She only comes out of her room to use the exercise equipment when the room is closed. That was her first request of Mr. Doring. The use of the room when no one else was there." Meredith pursed her lips again. "She's so secretive, if Mr. Doring didn't go in and out and talk about her, I'd think there wasn't anyone there."

"What time does she go to the exercise room?" Ryan asked.

"Eleven at night till midnight." Meredith stuck her hand in her trouser pocket and pulled out a small phone. "Gotta go. It was good seeing you, Shandra."

"You too. Can't wait to work with you on the art event this summer." Shandra smiled at the woman. She did enjoy working with her. Meredith got down to business and made sure the art looked its best while on display in the lodge.

Meredith headed down the hallway as Ryan stepped closer to Shandra.

"We can't hang out here all day, but we'll be back for a drink and dance in the bar tonight."

She nodded. "We need to see who this Mrs. Talridge is. It's kind of suspicious that she showed up the day Carl was found murdered and is friends with Tabby." Shandra had a feeling this woman could be the key to Carl's death.

***

Ryan could tell Shandra had high hopes of exposing the woman tonight. She'd been more animated and free since they'd arrived at the lodge. Woody eyed them nervously when they walked into the bar, but when they didn't approach him, he loosened up and sang a moving set of songs.

Shandra leaned toward him. "When do you think we should head to the fourth floor?"

He checked his watch. "In another half hour. Come on. Let's dance, that will use up some of our energy."

She smiled and stood. He took Shandra's hand and escorted her to the edge of the dance floor. They hadn't run into Doring or Ms. Vincent tonight. He hadn't ruled either one out as a suspect. Doring mainly because he didn't like the man, but Ms. Vincent because she had motive and means to get to the weapon.

Ryan held Shandra close as Woody crooned a slow song. Always vigilant, even while holding her, he spotted Pete and Stu standing in the bar doorway.

"What's wrong?" Shandra asked, raising her head off his shoulder.

"Pete and Stu just walked in." Ryan maneuvered them through the other dancers in the middle of the room to the side farthest from the main door. He shot a glance toward the door leading into the restaurant kitchen.

"We're going to duck out of here through the kitchen," he said in Shandra's ear.

She nodded toward their table. "What about our coats?"

He studied the end of the bar in relation to the kitchen door. "Stay here. I'll have the bartender pick up the coats like they were left behind by customers. He can hold them for us until we come back." Ryan slipped through the dancers to the end of the bar. He kept his back to Pete and Stu as he called the bartender over.

"My girl and I are going to slip out. Could you grab our things over at the table under the amber light?" He nodded his head in that direction and slid a ten across the counter. "We'll be back shortly."

The bartender palmed the bill and nodded.

Ryan noted the two detectives were headed toward Woody.

Back at Shandra, he caught her by the elbow and led her into the kitchen. Several people glanced up but no one said anything as they kept a straight line through

147

the kitchen and popped out into the dining room.

He kept on moving until they left that establishment and headed to the elevator.

At the elevator he hit the up button, held Shandra next to him, and waited for the doors to open.

The doors opened and two young couples walked out of the elevator talking like a flock of magpies.

Shandra stepped in, he followed, and punched the button for the fourth floor. The contraption whooshed upwards and stopped. The doors slid open and they stepped out. Ryan scanned the signage for the room they wanted. He led Shandra down the hall, noting the signs to the stairway, elevator, and stopping to read the map to see where the exercise room was located.

"Rather than wait here to see who comes out of the room and possibly be spotted by Doring or Ms. Vincent, we could hang out in the hallway by the exercise room. If she's the only one in there, we'll know it's this Mrs. Talridge." Ryan waited for Shandra's reply.

She smiled. "That's a good idea. If Sydney and Tabby frequent this woman's room, we shouldn't be hanging around here."

They returned to the elevator and went up one more floor. They stepped out, and around, several sweaty people waiting to enter the elevator.

Ryan nodded to them and led Shandra down the hall to the door of the exercise room. He checked his watch. "Ten minutes."

Shandra wandered on down the hall. "There's a bench here. We can wait and when we hear the elevator doors open we can figure out a way to not look conspicuous." She blushed.

He grinned at what she wasn't saying. Like they could use kissing as a way to not be seen. "That sounds like a good idea." Ryan walked down the hall and sat on the bench. He grasped Shandra's hand and drew her down beside him.

"Did you see that Pete and Stu were headed toward Woody?" she asked.

"Yes. I like the guy. I hope they didn't find evidence against him." He rarely felt sorry for a suspect but Woody was an exception. His family had gone through enough tragedy.

"They won't find any. If my dreams are correct, Carl was killed by two women." Shandra squeezed the hand he still held. "We have to find them before they decide Sydney, or someone else, is collateral damage."

"I agree. The way they tried to frame you, they aren't above killing more to make sure they don't get caught. Which makes me wonder if this Mrs. Talridge is part of the murder. You would think she wouldn't arrive the day the body is found and remain." Ryan had a hard time believing someone who hadn't been connected and didn't need to stay, would. Ms. Vincent couldn't leave because she was a suspect, but for someone the police had no clue about to remain—it didn't make sense.

The elevator doors swished open. Ryan pulled Shandra into his arms, tilted his head down, resting on her shoulder but keeping one eye on the hall. A tall, slender, blonde woman stepped off the elevator. He turned so Shandra could get a glimpse of the woman.

Her intake of breath told him she knew the woman.

A door down the hall clicked and Shandra pushed out of his arms. Her eyes were big and round.

"It's Alexis!" she said in a rushed breath.

"As in, Landers' sister?" Ryan now knew why the woman was keeping a low profile.

Chapter Twenty-one

Shandra had wondered if the woman in her dream was Alexis. The regal way she'd held herself, the blonde hair, and the fine clothing. But she'd hoped it wasn't.

"That was Carl's sister. Why is she here? Do you think the detectives know it's her?" Thoughts spun in her head and collided. Why would she kill her brother?

"I don't know. I'm going to text Cathleen and ask her." He started punching numbers then looked up. "Is Talridge her last name?"

"I don't know. If she married it could be. The last I knew she wasn't married." Shandra stood and walked toward the exercise room. She was positive it was Alexis, but she wanted one more glance to believe it.

She stepped up to the window, sucked in air, and backed away. That was why they wanted the room after hours. Did Sydney know?

A hand on her shoulder caused her to whirl around. Ryan peered into her eyes. His brow furrowed in concern.

"What did you see?" he asked.

"Alexis and Tabby kissing."

Ryan stared at her. "You're sure?"

Shandra raised a shoulder toward the window. "Take a look."

Ryan eased beside her and peered into the window. He remained longer than she had but backed away, his eyes wide and his face blank. "You're right. They're kissing and more."

"Do you think Sydney knows? And how can Tabby live with Carl, and from what Sydney said, sleep with him, and then do that?" She was confused beyond words.

"Let's go." Ryan grasped her hand and led her to the stairs. "They might hear the elevator open and look out the window."

Shandra was thankful for the sound of the metal stairs echoing in the enclosed stairwell. The sound kept her from thinking too hard.

They stopped at the first floor and Ryan shoved the door open. The stairs brought them outside at the back of the lodge. They stood in the cold, staring at the door into the lodge. Without a room key they couldn't get in.

"Come on." Ryan led her around the side of the lodge to the front doors.

Her teeth were chattering by the time he pulled the front door open and led her inside.

Pete and Stu walked toward them. Both men had a glare on their faces.

Ryan squeezed her hand and continued forward. "Detectives."

"We just had an interesting conversation with Woody York," Pete said.

"He said you two already questioned him," Stu added.

"We talked with him as fans of his music," Ryan said, stopping in front of the two men.

"And his sister. You aren't authorized to talk about his sister," Pete said.

"Shandra lived as his sister lived. We can talk to him about that experience," Ryan said. "Besides, he's not your suspect."

Stu stepped forward and shoved a finger into Ryan's chest. "You aren't in charge of this investigation, yet you are investigating people and telling us who is or isn't a suspect."

Shandra's heart clenched as Ryan's face turned red.

He released her hand and shoved the detective's hand away from him.

"Ryan. Don't." She grabbed his arm, settling it to his side. "Detectives. We just spotted Carl Landers' sister upstairs. Did she contact you about her deceased brother?"

The two glanced at one another.

"No. Why is she here? His body was to be sent to his mother when the autopsy was finished," Pete said.

"She's consorting with Ms. Vincent," Ryan added.

Pete pulled out his notepad. "What's her name?"

"I knew her as Alexis Landers when I met her eleven years ago. She's signed in here as Mrs. Talridge." Shandra pushed her hair off her face and stared at Ryan. "I'd like to go home."

He nodded. "Let's get our coats." He led her by the two detectives and into the bar.

The bartender handed over their coats. Ryan

walked over to the band and put a bill into the tip jar.

"Why did you put money in the tip jar?" She asked as they walked out of the bar.

"Wanted Woody to know we do enjoy his music and weren't just harassing him."

Shandra smiled. That was what she loved about this man.

***

Ryan sat on the couch next to Shandra. He enjoyed moments like this. But the silence right now had more to do with what they'd seen and not just a quiet comradery. They hadn't said much on the drive home either. What they'd witnessed had them both mentally scrambling to make sense of what they did know.

Shandra looked up from her cup of hot chocolate. "Who do you think is using who?"

He squeezed her leg. "I don't know what you saw, but it looked like Tabby was the dominate one."

She fell silent and sipped her chocolate.

His phone buzzed. He picked it up from the coffee table. A message from Cathleen.

Alexis Landers is still Alexis Landers. The Talridge name is made up.

"It looks like Ms. Landers didn't want anyone to know who she is while she's here." He tipped his phone toward Shandra.

She glanced at the message. "That puts her to the top of the list of suspects. The only reason you sign into a hotel with a name not your own is because you are up to something or hiding." She took another sip. "I don't think she came here to hide."

"Not when she was at Landers' place the day he traveled here." Ryan set his phone down. "She was giving herself an alibi. She probably already had her ticket bought to fly here from New Mexico, but wanted to make sure the housekeeper could say she was in Albuquerque the day before her brother's death."

Shandra tapped the mug with her finger. "Do you think she killed him or Tabby did?"

He shrugged. "I bet they were both in on it. Ms. Vincent playing Doring against Landers in the bar was to set up another person who could have killed him and it gave her a reason to leave the bar by herself."

"But where was Alexis? Could she have flown into the closest airport and driven here in time to shoot Carl?" Shandra set the mug down.

Ryan grabbed his laptop off the coffee table and opened it. "Let's see where the closest airport would be that would bring in commercial flights."

Shandra leaned next to him, peering at the screen as he typed. "What if she chartered a plane as Mrs. Talridge believing no one would know her as Carl's sister?"

He stared into her golden eyes. "The way you think, it's a good thing you're on my side."

She smiled and kissed his cheek. "I'll always be on your side."

Ryan wanted to shove the computer off his lap and gather Shandra onto it, but they had a murder to solve. "I'm contacting Aldo to check into charter flights leaving Albuquerque and arriving within a hundred miles of here."

"That's a good idea. Alexis has money. It wouldn't mean much to her to charter a plane. But I don't understand, if she and Tabby are working together, why did they blackmail the other women? Alexis doesn't need the money." Shandra rose from the couch and picked up their empty mugs.

"That is something to ask after they are arrested." He sent the email off to Aldo and watched her saunter into the kitchen. Dishes clinked and the refrigerator door opened and closed several times.

When she didn't return he wandered into the kitchen.

Shandra stood at the sink, staring out the window.

Ryan walked up behind her, putting his arms around her waist. "What are you thinking about?"

"Everything and nothing." She leaned her head against his shoulder. "I never had siblings, but why would you want to kill a family member?"

"I do have siblings that have given me more grief than I thought I could stand, but I've never wanted any of them completely out of my life." He laid his cheek against her head. "From what you've told me of Landers, his mother and his sister, their family has issues. Look what Landers did to you and all those other women. It isn't hard to imagine another member of the family could be unhinged enough to kill. Especially if that person felt wronged or vengeful."

Shandra shuddered in his embrace. "I'll never understand the need to take a life."

He had a pretty strong idea she was thinking of her stepfather killing her father. She'd had that kind of violence in her life and knew the tragedy for the ones left behind.

"I don't either. In my occupation, I have to weigh the safety of one over another."

"Have you killed someone?" Her voice was barely above a whisper.

His mind latched onto the alley in Chicago. All those young men who died or fought to stay alive after the gang that he'd set up the meet with had tried to gun them down. He'd lost several friends and nearly his own life that night. He hadn't pulled the trigger, but in the eyes of those still alive or related to the dead members—he had.

"While in the military, yes. We were trained to take out the enemy. As a police officer, I haven't killed anyone with my own weapon."

Shandra twisted in his arms. Her golden eyes peered into his. "What do you mean?"

He regretted what he'd just said. The less people who knew about his part in that tragedy the better. "Forget what I said." He held her tight and kissed her lips, hoping to draw her mind away from his words.

When Ryan came up for air, Shandra clung to him. He stared into her eyes and smiled at the heat he saw in their depths. Soon, he'd win her completely over.

Sheba woofed at the back door.

Ryan released Shandra and let the dog out. When he turned back to the kitchen Shandra watched him, her lips tipped in a slight grin and her eyes guarded.

"I'm going to bed. See you in the morning," he said and shuffled down the hall to the guest room.

Chapter Twenty-two

Shandra put the coffee on and set out a package of frozen cinnamon rolls before heading out to the studio. She'd awakened before dawn, restless and wanting to work on the vase. It wasn't so much her creative muse pushing her as the need to do something. They had to wait to see if Pete and Stu confronted Alexis and for Aldo to find out about the plane.

But the more she thought about Alexis and Tabby. And Tabby and Carl. And Tabby and Sydney. And Sydney and Carl. And Carl and Woody. None of the relationships other than Alexis and Tabby made sense. Why would Tabby put up with Carl's humiliation when she had such a strong personality? And why would she carry on with Sydney when she had a yearning for Alexis? Or was Tabby using them all—Alexis, Sydney, and Carl?

Woody seemed like the person who made the most

sense to have killed Carl. He had his desire to seek revenge for his sister. But he was either a pathological liar or he truly didn't kill Carl. She was leaning toward he didn't do it. Everything he'd told her and Ryan had sounded from the heart and not that of a person covering up the fact they'd killed someone.

The door opened. "There you are."

Ryan walked in with a tray, holding two mugs of steaming beverage, which, by the smell was coffee and a plate with steaming cinnamon rolls.

"If you weren't sure where I was, why did you bring out this tray?" she asked, wiping her hands on the rag hanging from her pocket as he placed the tray on the small table in her sitting area.

"I'm a detective remember? There was smoke coming out of the chimney." He walked over to the small pot-bellied stove she used to warm up the studio when she wasn't firing anything in the kiln. He opened the stove door and tossed another small log into the red coals and closed the latch.

She smiled. "I should have known I couldn't hide from you." She sat in one of the two chairs that flanked a small table by the front window. Until Ryan's recent stay, there had always been one chair and the small table. She picked up a mug, inhaled the scent, and then sipped. "How did you know I was ready for this?"

He sat in the other chair and grinned. "I'm a detective."

She laughed. "Don't get cocky, we haven't figured this one out."

"Yet." He picked up a plate with a roll. "We will."

"I've been thinking. What if Tabby is using everyone? What if she is the one who did the blackmailing, Carl found out, and she killed him, but to take the blame off her, she started the confrontation between Sydney and Carl. She could have also called Alexis here to have one more person who would make a good suspect." Shandra put the coffee down and picked up the warm plate with a cinnamon roll.

"We know the weapon was registered to Landers, which means it must have been in his possession, or whoever killed him, stole it from his house and brought it here. Ms. Vincent would have been the likeliest person to have access to the weapon, unless he took it up on the mountain knowing there might be an altercation between him and the person he was meeting." Ryan shoved a piece of roll into his mouth.

Shandra stared at him. "How do you know Carl was meeting someone and not that the two of them went out for some night skiing?"

He chewed the food in his mouth and said, "His skis were stuck in the ground like he'd taken them off and made a sign of sorts so he could be found."

"Did Cathleen say if Carl's phone records had been looked at?" Shandra set the plate down. "If he was meeting a person, then someone had to have called or sent him a message about the meeting."

"There is a request in to look at his phone record. But chances are slim it will reveal anything. For all we know, someone could have passed him a note or set up the meeting face to face."

She spun in her chair to face Ryan. "When I listened in on Sydney and Tabby at the diner, Tabby said Carl had his eye on one of the maids. We should go back to the lodge and find out who she is and have a talk with her."

He finished chewing and took a swallow of coffee. "That was just Ms. Vincent trying to make her throwing herself at Doring not seem so bad."

"No. I bet Carl was looking for someone he could manipulate. You said it yourself, Tabby wasn't his type. She was there for a reason, but I don't think it was to sleep with. She wouldn't have put up with his bedside manners." Shandra shuddered. She no longer needed to dwell on the time she spent with Carl but it would take even more years to erase all the shame.

Ryan placed their plates and mugs on the tray and picked it up. "It looks like we're headed to the lodge again today."

She stood. "Yes. I'll tell Lil and meet you at your pickup."

Balancing the tray on one arm, he reached out and rubbed a hand over her cheek. "You might want to come in the house and clean up a bit. You have clay smudged on your cheek and sprinkled in your hair."

"Okay, I'll meet you in the house." Shandra left the studio by the back door. It was a shorter route to the barn and the room Lil stayed in. The path through the snow was worn down and easy to walk.

She pushed the small barn door open and walked in. The sweet scent of alfalfa hay, earthy horse, and leather met her nostrils and brought her instant calming. As a child she'd hid in the barn with her horse when she felt misunderstood by her mother, stepfather, and her school mates. She'd been on the outside of that world and never understood why she felt that way. Not until the summer she turned thirteen and defied her mother and Adam, getting a ride to town and hopping on a bus for the reservation and her father's mother—Ella,

Grandmother. That summer had shown her what was missing, but she wasn't able to fully grasp that and her life until she'd left Carl.

"Meow." Lewis, Lil's orange cat wrapped around Shandra's legs.

"Hello, Lewis. Is Lil in her room?" She walked to the door of the tack room and knocked. She'd offered Lil the comforts of the small apartment above the studio many times, but the woman only used it for showers and washed her laundry in the house. She preferred the small room in the barn.

"Lil? You in here?" Pushing the door open, she found the room empty. "She must be out checking on the horses." Shandra headed to the door that led to the corral and set Lewis on some stacked bales. "That must be why you're in here alone. Too cold out there for your old bones."

She shoved open the double doors that led to the corrals beside the barn. She'd found Lil here earlier this winter having tried to climb a fence and broken a leg. This time she found her employee standing in the middle of the corral on packed snow, currying Lil's mare Sunshine.

"Sunshine looks appreciative," Shandra said.

Lil startled and twisted her head to peer over her shoulder. "Now who's sneaking up on who?"

"Ryan and I are headed to town. You need anything?" She leaned on the corral gate. Apple nickered and walked over, snuffling her, looking for treats. "Hey girl. We need to go for a ride even if it's short. I bet you're getting corral fever."

"I don't need anything but the truth." Lil wandered over to the gate. She patted Apple's neck and peered at

Shandra. "What was all that talk them cops were saying about tapes and such?"

Shandra forgot she'd told the woman she'd catch her up on the situation. With Ryan around she didn't visit as much with Lil. When there was just the two of them out here, they talked more.

"My past. There is a time I'm not proud of. I don't have time to go into detail, but I thought a man loved me—"

"That dead professor?"

"Yes. He wooed me and I fell. I was innocent and looking for acceptance from—"

"Your stepfather or a male figure like him."

"Yes. Anyway, he abused me until I found the strength to get away. I've found out he did that to many young women. It turns out he was videotaping the women with him while he humiliated them in bed."

Lil held up a hand. "I don't need to hear any more. Is that why those cops think you killed the professor?"

"Yes. But I was never blackmailed. I didn't know anything about the tapes until the woman who came here with Carl mentioned them in the diner." Shandra thought about that. The woman had said that loudly, to make sure others heard it. She was trying to make sure even Shandra's friends had reason to believe she'd killed Carl.

"I have to go. Ryan's waiting for me." She spun from the gate.

"Hey!"

Shandra pivoted back to the corral.

"I don't think much of cops, but Ryan will help you find the real killer."

That was high praise for a man Lil had disliked

from the first because he was a policeman. "Thanks. I know he will."

Shandra hurried around the side of the barn and straight for the house. If she cleaned up fast enough, they could go to the lodge, find the woman, and have lunch at Ruthie's diner. She was craving a caramel shake.

Chapter Twenty-three

Ryan parked his pickup in the lodge parking lot and started around the front to open Shandra's door. His phone buzzed. Aldo.

He grabbed her hand and led her to the lodge entrance as he answered the phone.

"What did you find?" he asked.

"There was a plane chartered from Albuquerque to Missoula last Tuesday. It left at noon and arrived in Missoula at four," Aldo said.

"Name of the person who chartered it?"

"Elizabeth Landers."

Ryan stood in the lodge lobby feeling like he'd been punched in the gut. The victim's mother had chartered a plane to Missoula the night her son was shot to death. They didn't need another suspect, they needed to be narrowing them down.

"Thank you." He touched the off button and stared at his phone.

"What did the P.I. have to say?" Shandra asked,

tugging him to the side of the lobby.

"You aren't going to believe this. He said a plane was chartered from Albuquerque and arrived in Missoula at four that afternoon. And the person who chartered it was Elizabeth Landers."

Shandra shook her head. "Elizabeth wouldn't have killed her own son. She doted on him. Alexis could have used her mother's I.D. and credit card to pay for the plane."

He stared at Shandra. Once again she came up with a scheme that he would have come up with eventually but it popped into her mind so quickly it astounded him. "True. Do they look alike? Enough to use her I.D.?"

"With all the scheming this took, I wouldn't doubt she bought I.D. with her photo and her mother's name." She nodded to the hallway leading to the offices of the lodge. "Let's go talk to Meredith and see who is or was cleaning Carl's room on Tuesday."

He fell into step behind her. She was a woman on a mission.

Shandra stopped at a door and knocked.

"Come in," called out a female voice.

She opened the door and motioned for him to follow.

A woman in her twenties sat at a desk, promotional materials were spread out across the desk. "May I help you?"

"We're looking for Meredith. Is she in?" Shandra asked.

The young woman glanced between the two of them and nodded. "She's on the phone."

"We'll wait." Shandra tugged on his sleeve and they both sat in the only two chairs in the small office besides the one the woman used behind the desk.

"Are you guests?" the woman asked.

"No, friends of Meredith's." Shandra plucked at the fringe on her shoulder bag.

Ryan pulled his phone from his pocket and texted Cathleen to check out the whereabouts of Mrs. Elizabeth Landers. If Shandra was correct and Alexis was using her mother's name and I.D., they could pick her up if the mother pressed charges. That would give them a chance to question her. If I was on the case.

"The light went off." The woman picked up her phone. "What's your name?"

"Shandra Higheagle."

"Ms. Gamble, there's a Shandra Higheagle here to see you." The woman listened and nodded. Hanging up the phone she said, "She'll be right out."

Shandra nodded.

Ryan's phone buzzed. It was Aldo again. "I have a call. I'll take it in the hallway," he said, moving to the door and out into the hallway.

"Did you find out something else?" he asked.

"They finally tracked down the pilot that chartered the plane from Albuquerque to Missoula. He wasn't willing to tell me who his passengers were. He said he was paid well to keep his mouth shut. It's going to take someone with more pull than a P.I to get him to talk."

Ryan didn't like the fact someone had paid the pilot to keep his mouth closed. "Did he tell you anything?"

"The person asked about renting a car and how long it would take to get to Huckleberry Lodge."

"Send me all the information in a report. Thank you for all the good work you've done." Ryan hit the off button as Shandra and Ms. Gamble walked out into the hall.

"I know this isn't normal, but we need your help," Shandra said, turning to the other woman.

"What kind of help?" Meredith eyed him before redirecting her attention to Shandra.

"Who was or is the maid in charge of the room Carl Landers reserved?" Shandra stepped closer to her friend. "I know that's an unusual request but Ryan and I have our theory of what happened to Mr. Landers. We think the maid can help discover the truth."

Meredith studied Shandra. "I've heard the rumors. That you knew him and he came here at your request."

"I did know him but I didn't ask him to come here. I hadn't talked to the man in nine years. I was as surprised as anyone else when I heard who had died on the mountain."

Ryan took this opportunity to step in. "Ms. Gamble, having a person die on this mountain on one of the ski runs can't be good for business. The sooner we find the person responsible, the sooner the rumors can be squashed and the lodge and resort will have the truth to tell people."

The woman's gaze moved back and forth between him and Shandra. "I honestly don't think you did it," she finally said. "If you two can find out who did and get things back to normal around here, I'd be grateful." Ms. Gamble pivoted and headed down the hall. "The maids are scheduled rooms by the head housekeeper."

Ryan captured Shandra's arm and followed the woman.

Ms. Gamble stopped at an open door. Lockers were along one wall and a long table with folding chairs sat on the other side of the room. A couple of college age women sat at the tables talking and sipping sodas.

The young women looked up and quickly started cleaning up the food wrappers and cans as they stood.

"Where is Mrs. Wilbur?" Ms. Gamble asked the two women.

They shrugged.

"She said something about checking on laundry," the sturdy brunette offered.

Ms. Gamble pulled her phone from her pocket and hit a button.

Ryan scanned the room and glanced at Shandra. She was studying the room as well.

"Gretchen, this is Meredith. Which maid was working the second floor northeast quadrant on Tuesday?" Ms. Gamble listened, nodded, and said, "Thank you."

"Jasmine Rimes has cleaned that section of the second floor all week."

"Is she here now?" Shandra asked.

"She should be." Ms. Gamble walked over to the two young women stowing things in their lockers. "Marcy, hand me your radio, please."

The thin redhead handed what looked like a walkie talkie to Ms. Gamble.

"Jasmine Rimes? Jasmine Rimes, location please?" Ms. Gamble stared at the radio.

Static crackled in the air and a voice said, "Two-fifty."

"Thank you." Ms. Gamble handed the radio back to the young woman and faced Ryan and Shandra. "Did you hear?"

"Yes." He headed for the door. "Thank you."

Shandra faced Ms. Gamble. "Thank you, Meredith."

The woman nodded and waved for them to go.

Ryan stepped out the door with Shandra on his heels.

Shandra was thankful Meredith had come through. She could have stalled and called the police, telling them she was investigating a murder, but she'd dealt with Meredith long enough that the woman knew she wouldn't lie or cheat.

In the elevator she studied the poster depicting a wonderful dinner in the lodge restaurant.

"Don't get your hopes up. Ms. Vincent could have made the whole thing up," Ryan said.

"I know. But it's the best lead we've had." She stepped off the elevator and followed the arrows to room two-fifty.

The maid's cart stood in the hallway between two-fifty and two-forty-eight. The door to two-fifty stood open.

Shandra knocked and entered the room. A woman in her early thirties with dark hair and a slender build turned from dusting the desk.

"Hello? You're not to be in this room," she said in broken English as she walked toward the door.

"Are you Jasmine Rimes?" Ryan asked, stepping up beside Shandra.

"Yes. Why do you ask?"

"I'm Detective Greer with the Weippe County Sheriff's Department. I'd like to ask you some questions about the man who was in room two-twenty-five."

The woman's eyes widened. "The one who died?"

"Yes. What can you tell me about him?" he asked, pulling out his notepad.

Jasmine's eyes widened at the sight of the book. "I cannot tell you anything. I know nothing."

Shandra approached the woman. "Jasmine. We aren't here to get you in trouble. We need to know if you noticed a note when you cleaned up Wednesday morning or if you overheard anyone making plans to meet with the man in the room?"

Ryan slipped his notepad back into his pocket and the woman relaxed a bit.

Jasmine shook her head. "There was no note. Just the woman's stuff all over the place. I told her, it is hard to clean a room when I spend all of my time picking up her things so I can do my job."

"When did you tell her this?" Shandra asked.

"That morning. She had ski pants hanging from the shower and other ski clothes hanging on all the chairs."

"Wednesday morning?" Ryan asked.

Jasmine stared at him like he'd asked her a stupid question. "Yes. Wednesday. They came in Tuesday. I didn't clean the room until the next day."

How could Carl have made a pass at the woman if she didn't come to the room until after he was dead? "Did you bring towels or anything to the room on Tuesday?"

"No. But Emilio, my brother, said he brought food to the room Tuesday night. He works in the kitchen." Jasmine glanced over her shoulder. "I must finish this room. I have more on the other side to clean."

"Thank you, Jasmine," Shandra said, tugging on Ryan's sleeve, pulling him out of the room and into the hallway.

He stopped out in the hall. "Every word that Ms. Vincent has said has been a lie."

"I know. I would bet my latest creation that she's the one who killed Carl." Shandra headed to the elevator. "There is no way Carl could have flirted with her. She didn't come to the room until he was dead."

"I told you, I wanted an appointment today." The voice speaking loudly down the hall was Tabby's.

Shandra stopped and peered into Ryan's eyes. "What do we do?" she asked in a whisper.

"I don't care if you are booked. Mr. Doring said I could have a massage today and I want one." The voice grew louder and closer.

Ryan pushed Shandra into the small alcove near the elevators. He put his arms up on each side of her head and leaned close, hiding her from view.

The elevator dinged.

"Get a room!" Tabby said disgustedly, and the doors swished shut.

Shandra peeked around Ryan's arm. They were alone. She released the tension that had tightened her body and stared at him.

He grinned and dropped a kiss on her lips. "I like hiding you."

Laughing, she shoved him away from her. "Let's go find Emilio."

They walked over to the elevator and pushed the down button. An elevator came from above, dinged and the doors opened.

Alexis stood against the back wall of the elevator.

Chapter Twenty-four

Shandra tried to hide her surprise and hoped the woman didn't recognize her. It had been over ten years since they'd met, and Shandra was more filled-out than back then. She smiled briefly and ducked under Ryan's arm.

He held her close and kissed her temple while waiting for the doors to close.

They swished shut and he pretended to whisper in her ear.

Shandra's heart raced, waiting for the woman to say something.

The elevator stopped at the first floor.

Ryan kept his arm around her, rushing them out of the elevator.

The click of Alexis' shoes on the stone floor stopped.

Shandra glanced over her shoulder and found the woman staring after them.

Recognition dawned on Alexis' face.

"She recognized me," Shandra said, as Ryan propelled her into the bar. "We can't sit in here. What if she follows and asks me questions?"

He kept moving through the bar and into the kitchen.

When the kitchen door banged behind them, she relaxed. Surely, the woman wouldn't barge through a door marked no admittance, unlike Ryan and herself.

"Is there an Emilio working in here?" he asked.

The dishwasher nodded toward a Hispanic looking man in his twenties.

Ryan captured Shandra's hand, leading her through the kitchen. He wasn't leaving her alone for a minute at this lodge. He'd also looked behind them and the woman had not only recognized Shandra, he'd seen the contempt on her face.

"Emilio?" Ryan asked when he stood five feet from the man chopping lettuce.

"Yes." The man turned to him with suspicion in his eyes.

"We were just talking with your sister, Jasmine," he said, to show the man they weren't here to deport him or cause him grief.

"My sister sent you to see me? Why?" Emilio set the knife down and gave them his full attention.

"We had questions about the man who was in room two-twenty-five. The one who died." He saw suspicion creep into the man's eyes.

"Why did she send you to see me?"

"She said you took food up to the man Tuesday night." Ryan released Shandra's hand and leaned back against the counter, crossing his ankles and arms.

Emilio didn't say anything, but his head bobbed

once.

"You look like food prep. Why were you working room service on Tuesday night?" He caught the way Emilio's eyes scanned the area to see if anyone listened to their conversation.

"When you do room service you are tipped. I don't get tipped cutting vegetables all day. If there are a lot of calls that come down, Tom lets me deliver. But that night. I knocked on the door. The woman answered. She wanted to know why I brought the tray. I told her it was called in. She argued with me that she didn't order it. I looked on the order. It was called in by Carl. She said, oh, and took the tray. But she didn't give me a tip."

"What was on the tray?" Shandra asked.

"A small pepperoni pizza."

She frowned. "Carl wouldn't have ordered that. He can't eat spicy foods."

"Did you put the food on the tray?" Ryan asked.

Emilio shook his head. "A new cook handed it to me and told me to take it to room two-twenty-five."

Ryan scanned the room. "Is he here now?"

"I have not seen him since that night," Emilio said.

"He had to have passed the note to meet on the mountain to Carl," Shandra said.

"Can you describe him?" Ryan asked.

"Tall, thin, shaggy black hair." Emilio turned back to his station and started chopping.

"What are you two doing in this kitchen?" Doring's voice boomed from behind them.

Ryan captured Shandra's hand and started for the door.

"I can have you banned from the lodge," Doring

said. His voice sounded like he followed on their heels.

Shandra pulled, but Ryan clung to her hand and continued to the door. She didn't need to confront Doring in his kitchen. Out in the restaurant, he led her toward the main entrance.

"If you two don't stop, I'll report you to the police," Doring said in just under a yell.

Ryan sighed heavily and stopped. He didn't need Doring complaining to Pete about him poking around the lodge under false pretenses.

"What do you want, Doring?" he asked, facing the man.

"I understand you've been lurking in halls, spying on my patrons, and asking questions of the staff." Doring smirked. "I know you are no longer on this case, and I could have your badge taken away."

"There are no laws against a person talking to other people," Ryan said, squeezing Shandra's hand. She shuffled her feet next to him and started to pull on his hand.

"It is if you are interfering with a police investigation."

Ryan inwardly groaned. Pete came into his view with Stu at his side.

"Mr. Doring, we'll take it from here," Pete said, nodding for Ryan to walk toward the entrance.

Getting caught asking questions had occurred to him, but the two detectives hadn't been hanging around the lodge before today, and he'd thought he and Shandra could get in and out without getting caught. That's what I get for being cocky.

"Let's have a seat over in that nice secluded seating area," Pete said, motioning toward the alcove Ryan and

Shandra had spoken to Meredith in the day before.

Shandra walked past him and sat on the bench in the alcove. He could tell she didn't plan to say a word. Her eyes were narrowed, her arms crossed in defiance.

"Pete, this isn't what it looks like." How many times had some perp said just that to me?

"It looks like you're conducting an investigation while you are on paid administrative leave. How would you like it to be unpaid and sitting in a jail cell for obstructing justice?"

"How can we go to jail for just asking questions?" Shandra spoke up. She'd planned to let Ryan do all the talking but so far they, she and Ryan, had dug up more useful information than the two detectives harassing them.

Pete shifted his gaze to her. "You're still a suspect."

"If you had enough evidence against me, I wouldn't be able to walk around and ask questions."

Ryan shook his head, but she wasn't going to sit around and wait for Pete and Stu to finally find the evidence.

"Have you asked Alexis what she's doing here? And why she used her mother's name to charter a plane to Missoula?" Shandra stood, placing her hands on her hips.

The detectives stared at one another.

Pete shrugged. "Ms. Landers says she came up here to discuss their mother with Mr. Landers, but he was already dead when she arrived."

"And she didn't tell Ryan she was here when he called telling her Carl was dead." Shandra nodded to Ryan.

"That's true. When I called to inform the next of kin, she made it sound like she was in Santa Fe and didn't plan to claim the body." Ryan pulled out his notepad. "Her comment was, 'I have appointments I can't break. I'm sure mother will take care of things.'" He handed the book to Pete. "Does that sound like someone coming to talk to her brother about a mother when she's passing the uncomfortable job of dealing with a deceased family member to that same mother?"

"For what it's worth. We didn't believe her. If she came to see her brother and he was dead, she should be back in Santa Fe comforting her mother." Pete handed the notepad back to Ryan. "What are you digging up today?"

"Someone had to have sent Carl a message to meet them on the mountain. We have been trying to figure out how and who." Ryan slid his gaze to Shandra. She nodded and he continued. "We found out a pizza, ordered by Carl, who didn't eat spicy food, was delivered to his room on Tuesday night. The person who delivered it said a new cook handed it to him to deliver, but he's not seen the cook since that night. That's over a week ago. Either the cook didn't work out and was fired that night or he wasn't a cook."

"Who delivered the pizza?" Pete opened the file folder he held and poised a pen.

"Emilio, a prep cook." Ryan said.

"Prep cook? Why was he working room service?" Stu asked, sounding skeptical.

"He has a deal with the head cook to do some room service deliveries for tips," Shandra said. It made sense to her. Everyone needed a little more money in their pockets over what a prep cook job would pay.

"Did anyone go through the hotel room after his death was deemed a homicide?" Ryan asked.

"We had to clear the woman out and then we went through it. Why?" Pete asked.

"That was what two days after the body was found? She could have thrown the pizza and note away by then." Ryan ran a hand along the back of his neck.

Shandra knew that reaction. He was frustrated and thinking. "Has the large dumpster outside been dumped yet?" she asked. If Tabby did throw the pizza and note out it would be in the dumpster.

"Wouldn't they have sent the food, tray and all, back to the kitchen?" Stu said.

"It would still be in a dumpster, but the one off the kitchen," Shandra said, not letting the deprecating tone of the detective rile her.

Pete pulled out a phone and punched a couple buttons. "Ms. Gamble, please."

Shandra was pleased to see Pete had discovered Meredith was the person to deal with at the lodge and not Sydney.

"Ms. Gamble, this is Detective Lathom. Has the kitchen dumpster been picked up since Wednesday?" Pete listened and his eyes lit up. "What time today?" A pause. "Thank you."

He shoved the phone in his pocket and turned to Stu. "Go put crime scene tape around the dumpster. The truck will be here in an hour to pick up the trash."

Stu hurried toward the lodge entrance.

Once he was out of sight, Pete turned to Shandra and Ryan. "I don't have a problem with you two investigating as long as you keep me in the loop." He stared at Shandra. "The only reason I've backed off on you is I respect Ryan and know he wouldn't harbor anyone he thought had committed a crime."

Shandra nodded. "Thank you. I'm glad you respect Ryan. I do too."

Pete shifted his gaze to Ryan. "Send me everything you've found out. You two running around like you are you're bound to draw attention from the murderer."

"I have it all in a folder on my computer at Shandra's. I'll send it to you as soon as we get back to her house." Ryan held out his hand toward Shandra.

She didn't grasp it. "Aren't we going to help dig through the garbage?" she asked.

"No," Pete and Ryan said at the same time.

"Take her home and keep her there," Pete said, pivoting and heading toward the lodge entrance.

Chapter Twenty-five

Shandra slurped the last of her caramel shake. She didn't even have to persuade Ryan to get lunch at Ruthie's. He'd suggested they grab a burger before heading home. Her chest felt sprung open when he called her house home. The more he stayed with her, the more it felt right.

"I wish we could have helped dig through the garbage," she said, feeling left out of the hunt for a note.

"No, you don't. I've had that job before. It's not fun." Ryan scrunched his nose and grimaced. "The smell takes days to get rid of."

A giggle slipped up her throat. "Do you think Stu is in the dumpster?"

Ryan chuckled. "That would be worth seeing, but I bet he's supervising from the ground."

"You two look happy," Ruthie said, gathering up the empty burger baskets. "Everything settled with that man they found on the mountain?"

Shandra shook her head. "Not yet."

Ruthie smiled. "But you two are having a fine time. That's all that matters." She winked at Shandra and headed to the kitchen.

"Do you think clearing me of a murder is a fine time?" she asked Ryan.

He grinned. "If you weren't a suspect I wouldn't have been able to spend this much time with you."

"That's true!" She laughed.

The bell over the diner door jingled.

She glanced over and her happiness vanished. Alexis scanned the diner and latched onto Shandra with her gaze.

Ryan was facing the same direction and scooted closer to her.

The woman strode across the floor in a sky blue coat, removing ski gloves. The swish of the ski pants she wore quieted when her snow boots stopped at the edge of the booth.

Shandra held out a hand. "Alexis, it's been a long time."

The woman swat her hand with the gloves. "Don't you dare act nice to me. You were one of my brother's whores and now you've accused me of his murder."

Before Shandra could gather her wits and hide the humiliation, Ryan slid off the bench seat and stood, backing Alexis away from the booth.

"There is no need to call anyone names." He flashed his badge. "If you didn't kill your brother, then why did you charter a plane to Missoula using your mother's name?"

She couldn't see Alexis, Ryan had expertly blocked them from one another's sight.

"I didn't charter a plane under my mother's name to anywhere." Alexis' tone didn't sound completely convincing.

She hoped Ryan heard the ping of fear in her words.

"How did you get to Huckleberry?" he asked.

"I flew and then drove."

Completely avoiding saying where she flew in to. Shandra wished she could see the woman's face to judge her expressions. She knew enough that to show her face to Alexis would get the woman's anger up and not get them any answers.

"Flew to where?" Ryan asked.

"I flew into Coeur d'Alene and rented a car." Alexis' voice came from farther away.

The bell over the door jingled, and Ryan sat down in the booth.

She stared at him. "Did she appear truthful when she said she didn't charter a plane in her mother's name?"

"She seemed more shook up than not telling the truth. As if she feared her mother being around. Which could mean Mrs. Landers is around here somewhere and was here before the murder." His brow furrowed.

"Where is she staying?" Shandra continued to stare into his eyes as if he had the answers. "I'm sure if she were at the lodge under her own name, Meredith would have mentioned it when we talked with her."

"How old is Mrs. Landers?" he asked.

"I would say close to eighty." Shandra thought back to when she was with Carl. His mother had seemed old then, but Carl was the oldest and he was near sixty at the time of his death.

"I wonder if she's still here." Ryan picked up his iced tea and took a swallow.

"Did you call her residence in Santa Fe when you called to tell her about Carl?" She could understand Alexis having call forwarding but not Elizabeth.

"It was her residence. An assistant answered and then Mrs. Landers came on the phone. You're right she sounded old." Ryan stood. "Ms. Landers acted like we were the first ones to ask her about the charter plane. If Pete talked to her, he should have asked her about it."

She took Ryan's offered hand and slid out of the booth. "None of this is making any sense."

The bell jingled and Maxwell entered the diner. He smiled, holding the door open for them to exit. "Take care out there. They say there's a storm coming this afternoon."

"We will. Thanks, Maxwell," Shandra said, stepping out into a flurry of snowflakes. "We need to stop at the store if there's going to be a storm. We're out of some things."

"I'll drop you off at the store and check in with Pete. I don't like the fact it doesn't seem like he talked with Ms. Landers." Ryan held the door open as she climbed into his pickup.

She watched Ryan walk around the front of the vehicle. A day like today she wished she had brought her Jeep too. Then she wouldn't have to wait on him to get home. She didn't like the large flakes and the way the wind tossed them everywhere.

Ryan slid in, started the engine, and headed toward the only grocery store in Huckleberry. Out of the corner of his eye, he noticed Shandra fidgeting with the leather fringe on her purse.

"I'll wait in the truck in the parking lot. I don't plan to hunt for Pete, I'll call him." He reached over, covering her hand with his.

"Thank you. I don't like being down here when a storm is coming. I prefer to be home."

"Most people would be worried about being snowed in on the mountain." He pulled into the parking lot. From the cars, it appeared everyone in Huckleberry had decided to stock up before the storm hit. He had to park in the row next to the road. But he backed in so he could watch Shandra walk to the store.

Once she was in the store, he pulled out his phone and dialed Pete. The detective's phone went straight to voicemail. "Pete, it's Ryan. Did you question Ms. Landers? When we saw her she acted like no one but Shandra and I had asked her about chartering a plane to Missoula. In fact, she said she flew into Coeur d'Alene. You might want to find out if Elizabeth Landers flew in the day her son was killed or if someone else did." He hit the off button and studied the people going in and out of the store.

A couple of older men stood under the eaves of the building smoking. Ryan figured they were either employees or waiting for wives. Movement to the right of the doors caught his attention. A tall thin person, with shoulder-length black hair stood with their back to the parking lot, staring into the store window.

Why would someone stare into a window like that?

The person stomped their feet and moved as if getting cold. His phone buzzed. Ryan glanced at the number and slid his finger across the screen.

"Pete, did you get my message?" His gaze went back to the store. The person with black hair was gone.

Shandra stepped out the door, two full paper bags in her arms.

"I did—"

"I'll call you back." Ryan hung up and started the pickup. There wasn't any sense in Shandra carrying the bags that far in the snow.

Blue streaked at the side of his vision, swerved into view, and headed for Shandra.

Ryan stepped on the accelerator as his heart lodged in his throat.

Shandra disappeared and the blue car roared out of the parking lot and down Lower Mountain Road.

Ryan slammed the truck into park, leapt out of the cab, and sprinted to where he'd last seen Shandra. She sprawled between two cars, her groceries scattered all around her.

"Shandra!" He dropped to his knees in the snow and fought the urge to pull her into his arms. Using all the constraint he had, he slowly checked her over for blood or broken bones. A purple lump started forming under her skinned forehead.

Several people gathered at the cars.

Ryan pulled out his phone and punched in 9-1-1.

"What's your emergency?" Hazel asked.

"Hazel, it's Ryan. There was a hit and run at the grocery store. Send an ambulance."

"Oh dear. I'll dispatch one right away. Stay on the phone."

He could hear her dispatching the ambulance.

"They should be there in five to ten minutes. Is the victim conscious?" Hazel asked.

"No. It's Shandra."

Hazel drew in a breath before asking. "Is she hurt

bad?"

"I don't know."

The sirens shrilled in the distance and grew closer.

"I'll call your sister as soon as the ambulance gets there."

"There's no need to do that." Ryan had survived his rehab after the gang shooting all by himself. He could get through whatever medical procedure Shandra needed alone as well.

The ambulance pulled into the parking lot, lights flashing and siren piercing. The EMTs made their way through the people and squeezed in between the cars.

"Sir, you'll have to move so we can treat her," one of the EMTs said.

Ryan nodded and stood. "Hazel. It was a blue sedan. I didn't get a license plate but the driver is a tall, thin male with shoulder-length black hair. He headed out Lower Mountain Road."

"I'll let the deputies know." Hazel hung up.

The EMTs had Shandra on a gurney.

Treat shoved through the crowd. "How'd that happen?" he demanded, glancing around at the gawkers.

Everyone shrugged and backed up as the EMTs carried Shandra and the gurney toward the ambulance.

Ryan started after them.

Treat grabbed his arm. "What about the food and your truck?" he asked.

"I need to go with her," Ryan said, thinking if the person missed this time, they'd be back to try again.

"Okay. I'll gather the food and bring your truck to the medical center." Treat slapped him on the back.

"Thanks."

Ryan climbed into the back of the ambulance after flashing his badge. The sirens started up, sending his hair follicles dancing.

He glanced down at Shandra and clasped her hand. *Stay with me. We're just getting this relationship started.*

Thin man with long black hair. The description could fit a lot of people but Ryan didn't think it was a coincidence that same description was made of the person who might have delivered a message to Landers to meet on the mountain.

Chapter Twenty-six

Voices, footsteps, and whirring wheels floated in her ears. The antiseptic smell of a hospital registered. Shandra opened her eyes. Pain shot through her head and she clamped her eyelids down.

"Shandra? I'm with you."

A warm hand squeezed her left hand. Ryan.

"Where am I?" she asked, not opening her eyes.

"The Huckleberry Medical Clinic. Dr. Porter said your only injury is a bump on the head." A light kiss touched her hand. "You're lucky you only hit your head diving out of the way."

Events started flooding her mind. She'd walked out of the store, hoping Ryan would drive up and help her with the heavy bags. The pickup started up at the same time she'd heard an engine rev to the side of her and spotted the blue car hurtling around the end of the parked cars. When it swerved toward her, she'd thrown herself between two parked cars. And obviously hit her head in the process.

"Did you get a look at the car?" she asked.

"Not a plate, but I saw the guy watching through the store window. I think it's the guy who gave Emilio the pizza. Anyway, the description fits."

The swish of curtains, tugged her eyes open. Dr. Porter stood beside her bed.

"I'm keeping you overnight. Head wounds are not something to take lightly. I had Chandler set up a room for you to spend the night. He'll be your nurse."

Shandra smiled at the young man standing next to Dr. Porter. Like his brother Maxwell, Chandler's dark skin and black hair only emphasized Dr. Porter's pale complexion, white eyebrows and hair, and light blue eyes.

"I'll be staying too," Ryan said.

"This isn't a motel," Dr. Porter said, frowning.

"I'm not leaving. Someone tried to run Shandra over. I'll not leave her here alone." He shot a glance to Chandler. "Not that she'll be alone, but I won't leave her."

"Ryan, I don't think anyone will try to hurt me in here," she said.

He stared at her. "I'm not leaving." His phone buzzed. He glanced at it and stood. "I need to take this."

She watched him walk only as far as the other side of the curtains where he could still see her.

"I have a feeling you won't be able to get rid of him," she said apologetically to Dr. Porter.

"I understand how he feels. Chandler, it looks like you'll have a patient and a guest, tonight."

"I don't mind." Chandler grinned at her and slipped a chart into the rack at the end of the bed.

"You have a pretty good knot and bruise on your

190

forehead. We'll keep you overnight for observation. Chandler will be waking you often. If your head gets unbearable ask for a pain killer. It's not prescription, just run-of-the-mill over-the-counter stuff." Dr. Porter glanced at his watch.

"Thank you. I could just go home and have Ryan wake me often and let Chandler spend the night at home." Shandra liked the idea of being tucked away in her own bed better than spending the night within easy access to whoever wanted her dead.

"Your injury requires someone qualified watch you." Dr. Porter nodded to Chandler. "If you have any problems call. My aunt needs her evening meds."

"Will do, Doctor." Chandler waited until the doctor was out of sight and said, "What would you like for dinner? I'll call over to Ruthie's and have Maxwell bring it by."

She glanced at Ryan still talking on the phone within sight but out of hearing. "You could send Ryan to get it."

Chandler picked up her wrist and stared at his watch. After setting her hand down, he shook his head. "I don't think he'll leave you here alone. Most men get overprotective when their woman is injured."

Shandra had to agree. She didn't think Ryan would leave her long enough to walk two blocks to Ruthies. "Soup for me. Whatever Ruthie has cooking will be fine."

"That's a good choice considering you have a head injury. Sometimes that can upset your stomach." Chandler continued checking her vital signs, and she stared at Ryan trying to figure out who he was talking to and what about.

Ryan squeezed the phone so tight he feared it might break. "What do you mean no one caught up to the car? He probably doubled back to see if he accomplished killing Shandra. Is Blane out looking for the car?"

"Do you know how many blue sedans are in Huckleberry?" Marlow, chief of the Huckleberry Police asked. "We can't pull over every person driving a blue sedan."

"I know." Ryan slid his finger across the screen and picked up the call coming in.

"How is Shandra?" his mom asked.

"How did you find out? Never mind. Hazel." He should have known the woman would call Cathleen, who would call mom.

"It's a head injury. They're keeping her overnight at the clinic in Huckleberry." He rubbed a hand across the back of his neck. His tense muscles ached.

"Do you want me to keep you company?"

"No. They aren't too happy I'm spending the night in the clinic. Mom, someone tried to run her down in the grocery store parking lot. I can't leave her alone." Tears burned behind his eyes. He'd kept a strong front for Shandra, but knowing his mom understood how vulnerable he felt at this moment, he let his emotional guard down.

"If it's just a concussion she'll be fine, and the two of you are going to figure out who it is before they can do anything else. You're a good team." Mom's no-nonsense chatter pulled him back together.

"Thanks. I need to make another call."

"Tell Shandra we're all thinking of her."

"I will and thanks again. I needed your wisdom."

He hoped his voice sent her the hug he wanted to give.

"You know you can always count on your family."

The phone went quiet. Family. He had that in spades and was glad of it.

He punched Pete's number.

"Wondered when I'd hear back from you. Sounds like you had some excitement." Pete's voice was overfriendly.

"If you can call having the woman you love nearly run over by a car, excitement, then yeah, I've had tons of it." Ryan wasn't in the mood to make small talk. "They haven't found the car or the man. He fits the description Emilio gave us of the person who sent a pizza to Landers' room. Did you find anything in the dumpsters?"

"Nothing that could be evidence but there was writing on the back of the room service receipt. Bear Run midnight. Which according to your report is the run where the body was found."

Shuffling papers whispered in the phone as he watched Shandra slide from the emergency room bed into a wheelchair. Chandler was moving her to a room.

Ryan followed and asked, "Did you discover who flew into Missoula on a plane chartered by Mrs. Landers?"

"We have a Montana detective inquiring. You think the victim's mother has been here the whole time?" Pete asked.

"I don't know what to think. I know when I notified her a servant answered and an elderly sounding woman came to the phone and stated she was Elizabeth Landers." He replayed the call and was certain the woman on the other end was the mother, but thinking back, she hadn't seemed the least bit surprised.

"We'll know more tomorrow. And for what it's worth. I don't think Ms. Higheagle killed Carl Landers. She's too smart to have left the trail we've been finding." The phone went dead.

Ryan nodded. Finally. He'd stopped outside the room Chandler had rolled Shandra into. He put away the phone and stepped inside.

"Put this gown on and I'll phone Ruthie and let her know what you'd like for dinner." Chandler faced Ryan. "What can I have Maxwell bring over for you?"

"Whatever Shandra's having will be fine." He stepped around the nurse.

"You sure," Chandler asked from behind him. "She only wants soup."

"Yes. I don't think I could eat more than that." Ryan replied. The squeak of the man's shoes on the clean floor faded.

"Let me help you." He pulled off Shandra's boots and socks, placing them over by a small counter. Her coat and purse hung on the back of the wheelchair. He grabbed the two pieces and draped them over a hook on the wall. When he turned back around, Shandra had the gown over her torso and her arms. Her shirt and bra lay on the bed. He picked those up hanging them over her coat. Turning back around, she held her jeans out to him. He hung those over the other clothes.

"Get in bed." He held the sheets back as she sat and slid her legs under the covers.

"I hate staying here, but I'm happy you're with me." She held out a hand.

Ryan grasped it and sat on the edge of the bed. "I wouldn't be anywhere else. I know you want to go

194

home, but this medical center is actually safer. After six the front doors will be locked and no one will be able to get in without setting off all kinds of alarms."

"I know, but my bed would be more comfortable, and I didn't tell Sheba I wouldn't be back tonight. She's going to worry." Shandra sucked in air. "Lil. We need to call Lil and let her know."

"I'll get your phone. If she hears your voice she'll be less likely to come charging down the mountain." Ryan walked over to where he'd hung all of Shandra's belongings and grabbed her purse. He placed it in her lap.

She dug into her purse, pulled out her phone, and punched a number. "Lil, it's me."

She listened, grinned, and said, "I won't be back tonight." A pause. "No. There was an accident. I'm at the medical center." She scrunched her eyes. "No. You don't need to come down. Ryan is with me. We'll be back tomorrow morning. They're only keeping me overnight because I hit my head." She listened. "Keep Sheba in the barn with you and lock everything up. Be wary of any strangers." Shandra rolled her eyes. "Yes, the accident was caused by someone else." She glanced at him. "He did all he could. And no, he isn't the cause of the accident."

Ryan shook his head. Crazy Lil would never be friendly toward him and always accuse him of hurting Shandra.

Shandra shoved her phone back in her purse. "Lil will take care of things."

"But she accused me of your accident." He grabbed the purse and put it back on the hook.

"You know Lil, she blames all law enforcement for

everything." She patted the bed. "I'm glad you were there today. Once they missed me, whoever it was may have jumped out and done more." She shivered.

He sat on the bed and pulled her into his arms. He'd wanted to do it since seeing her lying in the snow. "I'm glad I was there. They haven't found the car. But Pete no longer thinks you killed Landers, and they have a Montana detective looking into who actually chartered that plane to Missoula." He kissed the top of her head and continued to hold her. He'd never been as scared for anyone as he'd been seeing that car headed for Shandra and then finding her unconscious.

"There is something we're missing." She laid her head on his shoulder, her arms wrapped around him.

"I don't understand why you were targeted. We've both been digging and asking questions," he said, enjoying the closeness.

"Maybe this has more to do with Carl's family and not so much his past," she muttered against his shoulder.

Chapter Twenty-seven

Maxwell visited for an hour after he delivered the food from Ruthies. Shandra liked the man, but her head was pounding after all the questions she and Ryan had bounced back and forth wondering about Carl's family and how that might be what got him killed and not so much the blackmail and women.

"I swear if Ruthie and I don't marry soon, people are going to think something is wrong with me," Maxwell said and nodded to Ryan. "Same with you man. You keep living at Shandra's place and people are going to wonder why you two aren't tying the knot."

"We both have our reasons," Shandra said.

"I may be staying at her house and have feelings for her, but neither one of us is ready to commit to marriage." Ryan glanced at her and captured her hand. "We both have some demons from our past we have to exorcise."

This was the first time Ryan had mentioned he had a past that might get in the way of their relationship. If she could still think straight when Maxwell left, she'd ask what he meant.

Chandler stepped through the door. "Maxwell, you need to leave. I have to take vitals and settle my patient for the night."

Maxwell stood. "Vitals, my patient. Don't he sound all medical? Still can't believe my baby brother is a nurse. Should have guessed though, the way he always brought home injured animals." He slapped Chandler on the back. "Glad you're keeping people alive. Working with the dead isn't fun, but it helps the people left behind."

"Thanks for the grub, Treat," Ryan said.

"Yeah, thanks." Shandra could barely keep her eyes open. The light made the pain worse.

"No problem. I always bring Chandler dinner when he works nights." The sound of his heavy footsteps proved he left the room.

"Sorry it took me so long to shove him out. I had an emergency call and had to talk a mother through how to get a small toy out of her son's nose." The humor in Chandler's voice made Shandra smile. He loved his job.

"I could use that pain medicine Dr. Porter promised." She didn't open her eyes.

"I brought some with me. I figured you'd need it after my brother left."

Ryan chuckled and grabbed her hand. She squeezed, her thank you for his comfort.

She opened her eyes. Chandler propped her up with his arm as he handed her a little paper cup with pills. She tossed them into her mouth and followed with the water, Ryan held for her. "Thank you."

Chandler eased her back down and started taking her vital signs.

She closed her eyes and waited for the pills to kick in.

Ryan didn't like Shandra's pale complexion. But he wasn't going to say anything where she could hear. He eased out of her hand as Chandler put the blood pressure cuff on her arm.

They'd talked about the little bit she knew of Carl's family. Once Chandler left, Ryan planned to contact the P.I. and have him do a full investigation into the Landers family. Something had to pop that would shine a light on who killed Landers and why. He didn't think it was a coincidence that Landers came to Huckleberry. Someone orchestrated it to pin his murder on Shandra. But why?

Chandler finished, lowered the lights in the room, and headed to the door.

Ryan followed. Out in the hall, he asked, "Is it typical for someone with a head injury to be so pale?"

"It's the pain. I'm sure she has a monster of a headache. The best thing for her is to sleep. Sleep is nature's best medicine." Chandler slapped him on the back. "She'll be back to normal tomorrow."

"Thanks." Ryan stared at the bed and Shandra's sleeping form. Rest was the best medicine. He reentered the room, picked up the chair, and carried it out into the hall. Placing the chair beside the open door, he sat down and pulled out his phone.

The light was bright as he turned the phone on. He slid his finger across the screen and scrolled for Aldo's number. He found it and hit dial.

Several rings before the man's voice answered,

"Hello."

"This is Ryan Greer. I need you to dig up everything you can on Elizabeth Landers, Alexis Landers, and Carl Landers." He hoped this new direction helped them solve the murder.

"I sent you another email with more information on Tabitha Vincent. You might find it interesting. Especially where she was living before moving in with the deceased."

"I'll take a look at it. And we need the information on the family as quickly as you can get it. There's been an attempt on another person's life." A tremor rolled down his spine. Nothing could happen to Shandra. She had too much art to give the world and had given him a new meaning to his life.

"I'll start right away."

The phone went silent.

Ryan didn't have his laptop. He'd left it at Shandra's. As much as he hated reading the tiny print on his phone, it looked like that was what he'd have to do. He moved through the apps, accessed his email, and opened the message from Aldo.

Scanning the document on Ms. Vincent, he wasn't shocked to see she'd been a resident of the home for abused and battered women that Ms. Benham worked for. Everything seemed to circle back to the attorney. This may be the first time, Shandra's belief in someone was wrong.

***

Shandra woke. Her head wasn't playing drums anymore. She lay on her side and something pressed against her back. Waking a bit more, she realized there was weight over her body at her waist.

"Hey, I offered you a gurney last night."
Chandler's voice caused the person pressed against her
to jolt upright.

That's when the dawning came. Ryan had laid
down on the bed with her sometime during the night.

"Good thing I came in before Dr. Porter gets here.
He doesn't like more than one patient per bed."

Shandra giggled and rolled to her back.

Ryan sat on the edge of the bed, scrubbing his face
with his hands. "That gurney isn't comfortable," he
said.

She twisted to ease the kinks in her back. "Neither
is this bed."

Ryan grinned at her. "But the company made it less
uncomfortable."

Her cheeks heated, and Chandler chuckled.

"Come on, off the bed. Go in the restroom down
the hall and wash up." Chandler waved Ryan to the
hall. "You, my lady, can use the facilities. When you
come back out, I'll check your vitals. I'd tell you to get
dressed but that would be diagnosing and that's best left
to the doctor."

She grinned at Ryan's retreating back and then
Chandler. "Thank you for letting Ryan sleep on the bed.
He needs his rest." She slipped out of bed and headed
for the restroom off her room.

"I figured he'd end up there before the night was
over. It takes almost losing someone to really know
what they mean to you." Chandler closed the door to
the restroom.

Shandra contemplated the nurse's words as she
stood staring into the mirror. While she didn't like
being accused of murder, this had brought her and Ryan

closer together. Focusing her attention on the reflection in the mirror, her gaze latched onto a large square adhesive bandage over the tender spot on her head. I must have scraped my head as well as made the lump. She took care of business and discovered Ryan sitting in a chair, staring at his phone when she returned to the bed.

The scowl on his face made her wonder what he could be reading.

"What's so awful on your phone?" she asked.

He glanced up. "It's not awful but confusing." He shoved the phone in his pocket and smiled. "Your color is much better this morning."

"The pounding in my head no longer sounds like amplified war drums." She glanced over at her clothes. "Chandler made a comment I could dress, but he'd get in trouble for diagnosing." She walked over and grabbed the clothing off the hook. "I'll just tell Dr. Porter, I'm fine and ready to leave."

"Good idea." Ryan pulled his phone back out. "I'll be here."

She stopped at the restroom door and asked, "Are you going to share what you're learning?"

"Yes. Go on." He didn't look up, just waved with his hand.

She entered the restroom and dressed quickly. Exiting, she found Ryan in a conversation with Dr. Porter.

"I heard that man on the mountain was murdered. I didn't see that," Dr. Porter said.

"The cold and means wasn't noticeable at first," Ryan replied.

"Hope you solve this soon. Bad publicity for the

ski resort means less dollars pumped into the Huckleberry economy." Dr. Porter turned when the restroom door clicked. "Detective Greer told me you were changing. How's the head this morning?"

Dr. Porter motioned for her to sit on the bed.

She complied, dangling her feet a few inches off the floor. "It feels more like a normal headache and not so pounding."

"Good. Chandler said you didn't show any signs of a concussion so you are free to leave this morning. But take it easy for a couple of days. Head injuries are nothing to take lightly." Dr. Porter pulled out a small flashlight and examined her eyes.

"We'll head back to Shandra's place as soon as you give her the all clear," Ryan said.

Dr. Porter turned to him. "You might want to check with your deputies. We received a foot of snow last night. Not all the roads have been cleared."

Shandra glanced at Ryan. "I don't want to stay down here."

He shrugged. "We may not have a choice. I'll call dispatch and see what's going on."

She watched him punch numbers on his phone and walk out into the hall. Being in town made her feel vulnerable. She'd nearly been run over in the store parking lot. Where else would someone attack her? Sitting locked in her own house was the only way she'd feel secure until they figured out the killer.

"I'll send Chandler in with papers to sign you out. Take the over-the-counter pain medicine if your head becomes unbearable. Rest. That's the best cure for a head injury." Dr. Porter held out his hand.

Shandra shook. "Thank you."

He nodded and passed Ryan coming into the room.

"We're stuck down here until late afternoon. One of the snowplows is broke down so it's going to take longer to get the roads cleared. Since the upper mountain road is used by fewer people, it will be the last to be plowed." Ryan grabbed her coat. "Let's get breakfast at Ruthie's, and we can figure out where to hole up after that."

She didn't like the idea of hanging out in Huckleberry. "What is the road like to Warner?"

Ryan stopped shuffling her toward the door and stared at her. "You want to go to my place?"

"I'd feel safer there than hanging out here." She walked out the door. "Here someone is trying to kill me."

Chapter Twenty-eight

Ryan couldn't argue with Shandra's conviction someone in Huckleberry wanted her dead. He'd enjoy keeping her in Warner with him, but they needed to stay here. Where the killer was lurking. It was the only way to get this mess over with.

Shandra signed all the papers, and he opened the door to the white world of Huckleberry. Someone, probably Chandler, had shoveled the sidewalk in front of the clinic and leading to the parking lot. He spotted his pickup parked closest to the sidewalk. Chandler had made paths to both sides of the vehicle.

Treat had handed Ryan's keys to him when he brought their dinner. Unlocking the passenger door, Ryan helped Shandra in and went around to the driver's side. He would have come out and warmed the vehicle up, but he didn't want to leave it unattended while he brought Shandra out.

He slid in and started the motor.

"You aren't taking me to Warner are you?"

Shandra said, her voice full of defeat.

He reached over and grasped her hand. "No. Running to Warner takes us away from the people we need to catch." He kissed the back of her hand. "I promise. I won't let anything happen to you. Now that I know they are targeting you, I'll not let you out of my sight."

He pulled out of the parking lot and onto the street. Ruthie's was only two blocks away but he wanted the pickup close by for an emergency. At the diner, he parked in front where they could keep an eye on the vehicle from a booth at the front window.

Shandra stepped out of the pickup before he made it to her side.

"Wait for me," he said, taking her arm and escorting her into the building. The place was busy for a Thursday morning. Ruthie and her waitress were flitting everywhere.

Ryan propelled Shandra to the only open booth by a front window. He motioned for her to sit and slide over. He sat on the same side.

Ruthie hustled over to the booth. "Honey, Maxwell told me what happened. Are you okay?" Her brown eyes shone with empathy as she filled their cups with coffee.

"I'm fine." Shandra smiled at Ruthie.

Ryan didn't see the usual sparkle in Shandra's eyes. She wasn't fine. She was scared.

"She'll be better when I can get her home," he said.

"I heard one plow is down. It figures. When Mother Nature decides we need more snow a piece of machinery would stop working." Ruthie pulled an order pad from her apron pocket. "What can I get you this morning?"

"I'll have my usual," he said.

Shandra glanced at him. "You eat breakfast here so often you have a usual?"

"You have to admit, I have stayed here a lot the last eight or nine months." Ryan captured her hand.

"I guess so. I'll have scrambled eggs with cheese, please," Shandra said.

"Any fruit?" Ruthie asked.

"No. I'm not sure I can eat all the eggs." Shandra picked up her coffee cup and sipped.

"I'll have that right out." Ruthie headed to the kitchen with their order.

Ryan put his arm around Shandra and pulled her close. They had a lot to talk about but there were so many people in the diner they'd have to either shout to be heard or lean close. He liked the lean close version.

He turned his head and said quietly, "I've been reading the information Aldo put together on the Landers family."

She faced him. "Do you know who killed Carl?"

"Not yet. We're going to have to use the information I have to try and make the person show themselves."

"What did you find?" She picked up her coffee and sipped.

He continued to hold her close and speak in her ear. "Ms. Vincent was a resident of the women's abuse center where Ms. Bellham worked. She lived there up until six months before she started living with Carl. She seems to have vanished for the six months in between. But Mrs. Landers' housekeeper says a blonde fitting Ms. Vincent's description showed up to the house once with Ms. Landers."

"Do you think Alexis took Tabby from the resident home and they became lovers?" Shandra gazed into his eyes.

"I don't know about the lovers, but Aldo did confirm Ms. Vincent was seen several times with Ms. Landers before she moved in with Carl Landers." He released Shandra as Ruthie came their way with plates and more coffee.

"What are you going to do if you can't get home?" Ruthie asked, setting the coffee pot on the table and placing the plates in front of them.

"Oh! I should call Lil." Shandra bumped his hip. "I don't like talking where I disturb everyone."

Ryan gazed in her eyes a moment before he slid out of the booth. "Where are you going?"

Shandra shot a glance toward the door.

"Nope. How about back there by the restrooms? That way I can keep an eye on you. Outside, it's too easy for someone to harm you." He waited what felt like an hour for her to make up her mind.

"I'll go by the restrooms." Shandra didn't like standing by the restrooms to talk but she had to agree with Ryan about standing out on the sidewalk talking on the phone. She would be an easy target. Kind of like walking through a parking lot with two big bags of groceries.

She took a spot as far away from the people in the last booth as she could get without actually stepping into the hallway that led to the restrooms. Punching in Lil's number, she hoped the woman wasn't already out clearing the road to the house. If she was, she wouldn't hear her phone.

"Hello?" Lil answered.

"Hi Lil. I'm out of the clinic. Ryan and I are having breakfast. We heard there's a broken down snow plow so Upper Mountain Road won't get plowed until late today. How much snow did we get?"

"I just started up the tractor to plow. We have a good two feet at the house. Figured I'd need to clear it out, so you could get home."

"I want to come home. But it looks like we're stuck here until later today."

"That truck of Ryan's will only push snow so far and it will quit." Lil always had to find a way to put down Ryan.

"How's Sheba?" she asked.

"She was confused last night when you didn't return, but she headed out this morning jumping through the snow and into the trees. She came back with a glove. Far as I can tell it don't belong to either of us. If Ryan had feminine hands I'd say it was his." Lil laughed at her own joke.

"That's odd."

"That Ryan doesn't have small hands?" Lil asked.

Shandra chuckled. "No. That Sheba found a woman's glove. Did it look like it had been lost for a while?"

"No. It looks new."

"I'll talk to you later." She hung up and wandered back to the booth.

Ryan hadn't waited for her to dig into his food. He had half of his pancakes eaten. He'd slid next to the window and put her plate to the outside. "What's that perplexed look about?"

She sat down and picked up her fork. "Lil said

Sheba went for her usual romp in the trees this morning and came back with what looks like a women's glove. In new condition." Her mind swept back to the day Alexis slapped her hands with the gloves she'd removed as she entered the diner. "Do you think Alexis was in the woods behind my house?"

Ryan stopped eating. He picked up his phone and hit a button. "Pete. Do you have any idea where Alexis Landers is?" He listened. "You might want to find her. Shandra's employee Lil said Shandra's dog came out of the woods from behind the house this morning with a women's glove. We haven't seen it because we can't get back to Shandra's until they plow the road." Ryan stared at her. "How do I know it belongs to Ms. Landers?"

She shrugged. Ryan's belief in her dreams and her intuition were hard for him to explain to others.

"It's a hunch." He ended the conversation and went back to eating.

"Do you think he'll look for her?" she asked.

"We'll go to the lodge after we eat and see if we can conjure her up. In case Pete thinks we're a couple of neurotics." Ryan tapped his fork on the edge of her plate. "Eat."

Shandra started eating. The food in her belly eased the nausea from either the pain pill or her unease about Alexis. It was hard to picture the prim and proper woman as a cold blooded killer. But if she hid out in the woods in hopes of finishing off Shandra, there was little doubt.

"What else did you learn from the private investigator?" she asked, shoving the eggs around her plate.

"Landers had a son from a marriage that ended right before he started teaching with the Southwestern College of the Arts.

"Making the son how old?"

"Twenty-six. Aldo sent me a photo. He has black shoulder length hair and is tall and thin." Ryan didn't need to say any more.

"Like the person who slipped the note to Carl and the person who tried to run me down." Shandra flipped through her memory. "Carl never mentioned a son. I don't even remember him saying he was married."

Ryan scrolled through his phone and handed it to her.

She noted it was the information Aldo dug up on Carl. He'd started out at a different university. When several co-eds complained about his advances and one swore she was pregnant by Carl, he was let go. He and the woman moved in with Elizabeth. The baby was born and the Landers' money landed Carl a professorship at Southwestern College of Arts. It appeared he'd learned how to sweet-talk the co-eds and captured them into relationships. His wife divorced him and disappeared from the Landers' radar. Shandra knew the rest about his life. Her eyes locked onto the statement: "Elizabeth Landers procured the services of Malley Private Investigations to find her grandson, Ned."

Shandra glanced up. "Do you think it was Ned on that plane and not Elizabeth or Alexis?"

Ryan didn't commit. "We'll know whenever Pete gets that information. After reading this, I asked Aldo to see if he could find out what was in Mrs. Landers will."

"You mean with his father gone, Ned might inherit?" Shandra shivered. "But why go after me? I won't inherit."

"I don't know. Unless he thought you knew about him." Ryan shoved his empty plate to the middle of the table. He glanced over at hers. "Eat."

Shandra wasn't hungry. She thought about her grandmother's actions in the one dream. She'd gathered family to her. Was she talking about Elizabeth or just family in general that this was a family murder?

"I'm not hungry. Let's go to the lodge and see if Alexis is there." She hoped there hadn't been another murder on Huckleberry Mountain.

Chapter Twenty-nine

Shandra wanted to leap out of the pickup and charge up to the fourth floor and pound on Alexis' door. But Ryan insisted she not get more than three feet from him as he helped her out of the pickup and led her up to the lodge entrance.

A dark SUV with the license plate of the one Pete and Stu drove was parked at the no parking curb in front of the building.

"It looks like they took you seriously," Shandra nodded to the SUV.

"Or they are gathering more evidence against you," Ryan said with a smile.

"I thought you said Pete didn't consider me a suspect anymore." She shivered, thinking of how close she'd come to becoming a fatality.

"He did, but sometimes when a detective thinks they have the suspect they don't dig for any information other than what will prove that person did the deed. I thought Pete was better than that, but he's been working this like he has blinders on." Ryan opened the lodge door and drew her into the warmth.

Shandra loved this lodge. It felt welcoming the minute you walked into the warm wood and open beam lobby. Then she spotted the two detectives talking to Sydney.

"Why do you think they are talking to Sydney?" she asked Ryan and scooted closer to him as they approached the trio.

"I don't know." He squeezed the hand he held and continued forward.

Sydney spotted them first and pointed. "Ask her. She killed Carl, maybe she has a vendetta against the family."

Shandra's muscles froze. She couldn't move her feet.

Ryan faced her when she stopped. "You have two witnesses to where you were after nearly getting ran over. Come on. You're tough. No one can prove anything."

She nodded, swallowed the lump in her throat, and pasted a smile on her face.

Ryan smiled and they continued over to the detectives and Sydney, whose face was as red as the burgundy mat around the framed art behind him.

Pete took a step toward Shandra and Ryan, putting a barrier between them and Sydney. "Mr. Doring says Ms. Landers didn't return to her room last night. He thinks foul play is the reason."

"She killed Carl," Sydney said, pointing at Shandra.

Ryan released her hand. He made to step around Pete but the detective was ready. Shandra smiled at the

State detective. He'd known what Ryan's reaction would be to Sydney's outburst.

"Don't give him the satisfaction of me having to lock you up," Pete said only loud enough for Ryan and her to hear.

When Ryan nodded, Pete released him and spun around, facing Sydney. "I can guarantee Ms. Higheagle had nothing to do with Ms. Landers' disappearance. She was in the clinic all night since someone tried to run her down in the grocery parking lot yesterday afternoon."

Sydney stuttered a bit then turned to Stu. "What are you going to do about Ms. Landers being missing?"

"We need to search her room," Stu said.

"If she's not there you might want to check Ms. Vincent's room before you put her on the missing persons list," Ryan said.

The detectives turned their gazes on Ryan, but Sydney's gaze landed on the floor.

"Why is that?" Pete asked.

"Because we saw the two making out in the exercise room a few nights ago," Shandra said.

Pete glanced at Stu and the two turned narrowed eyes on Sydney.

"Did you know about this?" Pete asked Sydney.

"Yes."

"Have you checked in Ms. Vincent's room?" Pete continued to glare at Sydney.

"No. I mean, Alexis never went to Tabby's room. Tabby always went to Alexis."

Shandra didn't know how, but Sydney's face reddened two more shades.

Pete motioned to the elevators. "Do you have a key

to get into the rooms if no one answers?"

"Yes. I'll grab my master key." Sydney scooted behind the registration desk, where the young female desk clerk had been hanging on every word.

Sydney held up the key card, and they all loaded into the elevator.

Shandra stepped into a back corner and pulled Ryan close to shield her from Sydney's glares. If he was truly worried about Alexis, you would think he'd be staring at the numbers flashing by and not her.

Ding.

The elevator doors opened, and the group followed Sydney down the hallway.

He knocked on the door. "Alexis, it's me, Sydney," he called out.

No sound came from within.

"Open the door," Pete ordered.

Sydney slid the card through the scanner and pushed on the handle. The door swung open. The room looked as if no one had lived over a week in it.

"You two stay here by the door," Pete said, motioning to her and Sydney.

"Can I just follow Ryan," she asked, not wanting to stay with the man who detested her.

Ryan understood her discomfort. "I'll make sure she doesn't touch anything."

Pete stared at her and Ryan while Stu started opening closets and drawers.

"She doesn't touch anything, and you don't let go of her," Pete said.

"Thank you!" whooshed out of Shandra. The relief welling inside was so great, she could have kissed Pete.

Ryan grasped her hand tighter and headed into the

bathroom.

She concentrated on the items on the vanity. Using the back of his hand, Ryan slid the glass doors to the shower open.

"She's a neat freak," Shandra said, noting the bottles of face cream, shampoo, conditioner, and makeup all lined up by size and color.

"This shower looks like it's been cleaned. She hasn't been here since the maid cleaned the room." He led her out into the room.

"Her clothes are hung in the closet and they're neatly folded in the drawers. Her suitcase is sitting in the closet." Pete motioned to the open closet doors.

Shandra studied the clothing. "Something's wrong."

"What do you mean something is wrong?" Pete stepped beside her and stared into the closet.

"All her makeup is lined up by size and color. Her clothing is hanging by colors and type. But there's a cream-colored coat shoved between those two green shirts. Alexis wouldn't have done that. Someone else put that coat in this closet." She pointed to the coat that not only looked out of place in the color scheme but was shoved as opposed to hung neatly.

Pete put on gloves and pulled the coat out of the closet. A glove fell to the floor.

Shandra stared at the glove, trying to remember if they were the kind Alexis wore the day they saw her in the diner. Her mind flashed back and her gaze went to the closet. In the diner Alexis had worn a sky blue coat. This cream color would wash her out. It wasn't her coat.

"Are there two gloves there?" she asked the

detective.

He dug through the pockets, then bent and picked up the one on the floor. "No, just this one."

She locked gazes with Ryan.

Ryan had a feeling he knew where the other glove was. He didn't have a problem telling Pete since Shandra had two witnesses who knew she'd been in the clinic all night.

"Shandra's employee said Sheba came in from the woods with a new glove in her mouth that didn't belong to either Shandra or Lil." Ryan pointed to the coat. "Might want to bag that as evidence and go check on Ms. Vincent."

Pete nodded. "Stu, bag this up and take photos. We'll treat it as a crime scene until we find Ms. Landers." Pete strode to the door. "Take us to Ms. Vincent's room."

Doring jumped and headed back to the elevator. They dropped down two floors, and Doring led them to room 225. He knocked and called out, "Tabby, it's Sydney."

Pete motioned for Sydney to use the key card. The door swung open, revealing a room the complete opposite of Ms. Landers. Food wrappers, clothing, and towels littered the floor, the furniture, and the shower rod.

Sydney wandered into the room and spun in a slow circle. "Why did she trash the room?"

"This isn't the way the room usually looked?" Pete asked.

"No. She did have clothes on the chair and shower rod, but not the trash and look at the bed. The sheets and blankets are torn off of it."

Ryan couldn't stop the grin. Doring was seeing he'd been had. "When was the last time you saw Ms. Vincent?"

Shandra wandered into the bathroom. Ryan let her go. She knew not to touch anything.

"Last night after dinner. She said she didn't feel up to…" his voice trailed off and he coughed. "We'd been spending the evenings in Alexis' room."

Ryan had a feeling he knew what the pervert had been doing. "What about Ms. Landers? Did you see her?"

"No, she always ate in her room alone. Besides being a neat freak, she didn't like people watching her eat." Doring made a face like a child would to comment on a crazy person.

Shandra stepped out of the bathroom. "I think she left in a hurry."

Pete pivoted from where he was digging through the trash can laying on its side. "Why do you say she left in a hurry?"

"I've seen enough of her to know she wears a lot of makeup and is vain. All the makeup is gone except the under eye concealer that was half hidden by a wash cloth." Shandra waved at the room. "With the clothing strung out like this you don't immediately think anything is missing. But if you knew her wardrobe, I would guess she only took enough to fit in a gym bag or a large tote. That way when she walked out of the lodge it would only look like she was going to town."

Ryan stepped up beside Shandra and wrapped an arm around her shoulder. What she said made sense. He could tell Pete was thinking the same thing.

Pete faced Doring. "I want an audit for the use of

the key cards on these two rooms and any camera footage you have of the two halls and the lodge entrance."

Doring jumped. "I can get Meredith on the audit, but you'll have to talk to my head of security about the camera footage."

They left the room and stood in the hall. Pete called the Huckleberry Police and requested a man secure room 225 at the Huckleberry Lodge.

Down in the lobby, Doring led Pete into the office area.

Ryan captured Shandra's hand and led her toward the kitchen.

"Why are we going to the kitchen?" she asked.

"I have a photo of Ned. I want to see if it's the person who handed Emilio the tray he took up to room two-twenty-five the night Landers died."

This time they went through the dining room and into the kitchen through the serving door. Ryan spotted Emilio at the same counter, chopping up vegetables. He glanced up and scowled.

"What do you want? You two got me yelled at by Mr. Doring." Emilio didn't stop chopping.

"I want to know if this is the man who gave you the tray that went to the murder victim's room." Ryan opened his phone and scrolled to the photo. He held it up in front of the other man.

Emilio studied the photo for a long time. "It could have been him. But the chef who handed me the tray had a tat on his neck. I don't see one on that dude."

"He could have gotten the tattoo after this photo was taken. Does he look anything like the chef?"

"I didn't look that close. He has dark hair and is

thin. It could be him or it might not be." Emilio shrugged and went back to chopping his vegetables.

"What did the tattoo look like?" Shandra asked.

"It wasn't very big. I think a fist in a circle with a line through it. You know, like the signs, don't do this or that."

"Thank you." Ryan tugged on Shandra's hand, leading her out of the dining room.

"You have the look that says you have an idea," she said.

"We need to get to your place. I think I have the answer on my computer." He shoved open the lodge doors and strode toward his pickup.

"What if the road isn't plowed?" Shandra asked as he opened the passenger door.

Ryan climbed in behind the steering wheel and pulled out his phone. He punched the number for Pete.

"Yeah?" Pete answered.

"Have you made any progress with time frames there?" he asked.

"Not really. We know Ms. Landers left her room fifteen minutes before Ms. Vincent at eleven last night. Ms. Vincent returned at three this morning and left twenty minutes later and never returned."

"With the weather we had last night she couldn't have gone far." Ryan noted the piles of snow and the plowed streets. At three-thirty this morning the visibility would have been poor and the snow piling up. "Did she register a car with the lodge?"

Pete asked the question. Another voice, female muttered in the background.

"It looks like a small SUV. Probably a rental from Coeur d'Alene," Pete said.

"Or Missoula. Did your contact there ever confirm who chartered the plane?" Ryan just remembered he hadn't asked that question.

"According to the pilot it was a twenty-something, male, with shoulder-length black hair."

"You just described our suspect, but we're still trying to put a name on him." Ryan started the pickup, watching Shandra hunker into her coat. "We think he might be Ned. Carl Landers' son."

"Another family member?" Pete's tone said he'd had enough of the Landers.

"If Ms. Landers' missing glove is at Shandra's, we need a snowplow sent out that way ASAP so we can see if Ms. Landers is there as well." Ryan smiled back at Shandra's beaming face. He thought she might like that.

"I'll call county and tell them to send a plow that direction now." Pete hung up.

Ryan shoved his phone into his pocket. "We'll go sit in the feed store parking lot and watch for the snowplow."

Chapter Thirty

Shandra willed the snowplow to go faster. While waiting for the vehicle to start plowing County Road 15, she and Ryan sat in the pickup drinking iced teas and eating donuts. Now she had to pee so bad she held the seat belt and inwardly cursed every ridge of snow the plow made.

"I could stop and you could pee beside the truck," Ryan said after glancing her way twenty times in the last ten minutes.

"There's still five miles to go and the plow is moving so slow." She contemplated the time frame. "Stop. I won't make it."

She was unbuckled and the door opening before he stopped the pickup. She slid off the seat onto the plowed road and took two steps toward the back of the pickup, out of Ryan's sight.

Relief.

Standing and zipping her pants, she peered off the side of the road. Something blue sat among the white world.

She stepped up to the still open door. "I see something down off the road. It's blue."

"Climb in. I'll go check it out," Ryan said, pulling his revolver out of the locked glove box.

"I can go with you." She stood beside the pickup, not climbing in.

"No. You're still recuperating. Get in where it's warm." He climbed out of the driver's side and came around to where she stood. "Besides, someone needs to be here to explain why the truck is sitting in the road." He grasped her by the waist and lifted her into the truck. "Stay."

Ryan closed the door and climbed over the berm of snow on the edge of the road and disappeared.

Shandra sat in the vehicle warm and toasty, worrying about him. What if it was a car? Would Ryan be able to help them or did he need help? Just as she'd decided to follow, he reappeared.

He was covered in snow to his waist. Brushing off a bit, he climbed into the truck and held his hands out to the heater vents.

"What was it?" Shandra asked.

"A small SUV with rental plates."

"Tabby's?"

"We'll know soon enough." Ryan pulled out his phone, dialed, and spoke. "Pete, do you have the license plate of Ms. Vincent's rental?"

Shandra wondered where the woman was. If she or anyone else was in the car and injured, Ryan would have called dispatch.

"I found the vehicle. It's off the road about twenty-five miles down County Road Fifteen. No body or tracks to tell where she went." Ryan listened. "Yes. I'd say a search party would be a good idea. Also have county do a search of all the places along the road to see if she found help from someone." He listened some more. "I'll let you know."

Ryan shoved his phone in his pocket.

"Where do you think Tabby could be?" she asked.

"My guess is if she didn't wander out into the forest, she came back to the road and walked until she saw lights and headed for those. Who along here has lights you can see from the road?"

Shandra thought about all her trips up and down this road at night. There wasn't a single house on the road. Everyone lived on this road for the seclusion. "Maybe the Flanders house, that's a mile back toward town or Jess Metcalf's. He's about half a mile that way." She pointed on up the county road toward her place.

"We can't turn around and go back to the Flanders. But we can go forward." Ryan put the truck in gear and they headed up the road.

"At least the snowplow is ahead of us and we don't have to go so slow," Shandra said, looking on the bright side.

Ryan glanced over and smiled. "Until we catch up with it."

"That's true. There. That's the drive to Jess's place." Shandra didn't know many of her neighbors because only a handful stayed year round. Most of the places were vacation homes along the first twenty miles of the county road. From Jess on out the road they were locals who stayed year round. Jess, she knew well. He had a large hot house and sold her vegetables year round.

The drive was plowed, just as she would find her drive plowed once they reached it. Jess's two chocolate labs came bounding down the lane to greet them. Their pink tongues lolled out the sides of their mouths.

Ryan put the pickup in park as Jess came out of the large domed greenhouse. The sixty-plus-year-old man walked like a younger man. His reddish hair had turned white. Shandra wasn't sure but what he liked Lil. However, neither one of them would admit to it.

The minute the man recognized Shandra, he smiled and came to her side of the truck.

She rolled the window down. "Hi, Jess."

"Surprised you made it down the county road. Last I looked they hadn't plowed it yet." His gaze moved to Ryan. "This must be the fella everyone says is staying with you." Jess reached through the window extending his hand.

Ryan shook. "Ryan Greer."

"Pleased to meet ya. This young lady needs a man around. You never know who or what will come wandering in."

"That's why we're here," Ryan said. "Someone ran off the road last night about a half mile down the county road. Anyone come to your door for help?"

Jess shook his head. "Nope. When the snow started yesterday, I made sure I had plenty of wood for the stove and the greenhouse was buttoned up. Me and the boys hung out by the fire reading until midnight. No one came knocking."

"This would have been early morning. Around four."

Jess scratched at his hair line along the edge of his

stocking cap. "Charlie whined and stared at the window about five. I wasn't ready to get up and told him to go back to sleep."

Ryan opened his door. "You stay here where it's warm. I'll be right back."

Shandra rolled up her window as the two men met at the front of the vehicle. She opened her door and joined them.

"Did you happen to look around outside this morning?" Ryan asked.

"Just went straight to the greenhouse. Wanted to make sure it stayed warm and nothing was chilled." Jess stared at Ryan. "You think I had a visitor?"

"Do you have any outbuildings besides the greenhouse?" Ryan started walking toward the house. "And I'd like to look around the outside of the house."

Jess faced Shandra. "Why is he so worried about my outbuildings?"

"He's a county detective. The car off the road belongs to a suspect in the murder at the ski resort." She followed Ryan around the side of the house. Jess followed her, and the boys followed him.

Ryan stopped by a window.

There were footprints with dog prints over and around them.

"It looks like there were two people. There's two distinctly different treads." He studied the window jamb. "It looks like they were trying to get in through this window. See the marks dug into the wood."

Jess stepped forward. "Well, I'll be damned. You think Charlie whining scared them off?"

"Probably." Ryan moved to the back of the house, his gaze on the ground.

They followed the footprints, which led to a small outbuilding.

Ryan stopped her and Jess back twenty feet from the building and continued on his own in a half crouch, walking slow and soft. At the door he straightened. "Did you have snow shoes in here?"

"Yeah, I keep a pair for me and several for when my kids and grandkids come." Jess hurried forward. "Damn thieves!"

Shandra followed and saw the prints of two sets of snowshoes heading off into the trees. Headed toward her house.

Chapter Thirty-one

Ryan hustled Shandra back to the truck and onto the county road as fast as he could. He could tell by her silence, she knew the two people were headed for her place.

"If they were at Metcalf's place at five-thirty, they have four miles to travel by snowshoe to get to your place. Does anyone live in between you two?" Ryan asked.

"The Donellys. Tabby and whoever is with her would miss them if they walked straight to my place. The Donellys have a short driveway." Shandra pulled out her phone and scrolled. "I called Lil at eight. Do you think that glove was Tabby's and not the mate to the coat in the closet?" She stared at Ryan. "Do you think they were out in the woods while Lil was talking to me?"

"We'll know if things are okay in a minute. There's your drive." Ryan peered ahead to see if the road was cleared. "Looks like Lil was out here clearing the road. Maybe they're lost."

"Or they did go to the Donellys." Shandra leaned forward, her fingers gripping the dash.

The good thing about Lil plowing the snow, it made Shandra's drive smoother than the usual pot holes, rocks, and debris. She kept her driveway looking unnavigable to deter people from driving in.

Ryan sped along the drive and pulled up in front of the house. He leaned over, retrieving his revolver from the glove compartment. Shandra slid out of the vehicle and ran toward the barn.

He caught up to her, grabbing an arm. "Quiet. In case there is someone here, we want to surprise them, not us."

"Sheba should be greeting us."

A tremor ran down Shandra's arm. Ryan slid his hand down and grasped her hand. "Come on. We'll check the buildings starting with the barn."

They crept up to the barn and down the side to enter through the back door beside Lil's room. Ryan released Shandra's hand, gripped his revolver in one hand, and used the other to slide the latch on the barn door. He only opened the door far enough for them both to slip through. The barn was dark without any doors open or lights on.

Shandra tapped his arm and pulled him over alongside the wall of Lil's room. He moved along the wall, to the door.

With an ear to the crack of the door, he listened. No sound.

He turned the door knob and slowly opened the door. Darkness.

Shandra slipped in and was back in a matter of

seconds. "No one. Not even Lewis."

Ryan grabbed her hand and led her back out to the eye piercing whiteness of sunshine and snow. They stood a minute, blinking, before he led her to the back of the studio.

He entered cautiously and again found no one.

Shandra's eyes scanned the area. "It doesn't look like Lil has been in here this morning. The stove isn't going. She always starts the stove so we have heat to work in."

"Let's try the house." He led Shandra out the back of the studio. They crossed the open space to the back door and looked in.

"Lil cleaned up the kitchen," Shandra said, peering over his shoulder.

Ryan turned the door knob and stepped inside. He motioned for Shandra to stay.

He pivoted to the laundry room. The sound of water spilling into the washer gave a feeling of normalcy. With quiet steps, he continued down the hall and peeked into the guest room. Just his stuff as he'd left it. A few more steps brought him to the main room. His computer sat on the coffee table as he'd left it. Music came from Shandra's bedroom.

He crossed the main room and entered the bedroom with his revolver in front of him.

Lil shrieked, Sheba woofed, and Lewis raced through his legs.

Shandra ran up behind him. "Sheba!" The big dog shoved him out of the doorway, making her way to Shandra.

Lil threw a pillow at him. "You plum scared me to death!"

"What are you doing in here?" he asked.

"Getting Shandra's bed all clean and ready for her. I figured she'd need to rest when she got home." Lil turned off the radio, walked over and picked up the pillow she'd thrown at him, and tossed it on the bed.

"Why are you sneakin' in here?" she asked, pushing past him and walking into the main room, making the sppp, sppp, sound people do when calling cats.

"We were worried the two people who could be Carl's murderers were here. They stole snowshoes from Jess and their tracks were headed this direction." Shandra sat on the floor, her arms around Sheba's neck. She had been scared something might have happened to her big furry friend and Lil. Seeing they were both fine, she could let the tension that had been mounting release.

"I'm going to call Pete and tell him they are either at the Donellys or lost in the woods." Ryan pulled out his phone and headed to the kitchen.

"You should go crawl in your clean bed," Lil said, picking up Lewis and draping him over her shoulders.

"I'm not tired. Just glad to be home." Shandra stood. "I can't rest until we discover Carl's killer and where his sister disappeared to."

Ryan came back carrying a tray with cups and a tea pot.

"How did you get the water hot so fast?" Shandra asked, sitting on the couch.

He placed the tray on the coffee table. "Lil had a pot of water on the stove." He turned to her. "Thank you. Have some with us." Ryan sat down and pulled his computer onto his lap. "I have to dig through some files."

Shandra poured tea in the three cups. She and Lil sipped and watched Ryan.

His eyebrows scrunched together, then parted. His brow furrowed then smoothed out. Finally, he turned the computer to them.

She immediately recognized the logo. "That looks like what Emilio said the tattoo looked like on the guy's neck."

"It's the symbol for stop abuse." Ryan clicked some keys. "Ned has been an advocate against abuse of women and children. His name pops up on a lot of the documents with the women's shelter in Albuquerque."

"But if he's against abuse, why would he kill his own father?" She didn't understand how a person against violence could use it.

Ryan shrugged. "Sometimes the right switch is clicked in a person and they can do horrible things thinking it is for the best."

"Are you going to tell Pete?" Shandra asked.

"I can when he gets here. He's bringing a search team to start here and work their way toward town. The two in that car have to be out there somewhere."

"Where is that glove you said Sheba found?" Ryan asked Lil.

"In the laundry room." The woman pushed off the couch with her walking stick and thunked down the hall. She was back in less than a minute.

Ryan nodded for her to give the glove to Shandra.

She turned it over in her hands. "It's the mate to the one that fell out of Alexis' coat."

"Or someone else's coat," Ryan said.

"True. When she came to the diner, she had on a

blue coat. I didn't see that in the closet." Shandra thought about what they did know. "Do you think it's Alexis and Tabby who wrecked the car? They are the two who are missing."

Ryan shook his head. "Those two and Ned are the three possibilities. Or they could all be working together." He stood. "I'm going to have a look around outside. Lil, could you show me where Sheba came out of the woods with the glove?"

Lil stood and the two strode down the hall.

Shandra put her tea cup down and leaned back on the couch. It was good to finally be alone. She hadn't realized how much it meant to her until the last twenty-four hours. Sheba shoved her head in Shandra's lap.

"Girl, I missed you too. I guess I'm never truly alone." She closed her eyes. Even with the pain medicine, she'd slept in spurts last night. The warm room, Sheba's reassuring head in her lap, Shandra's eyes became heavy and she slipped into a light sleep.

***

"Go back in with Shandra. I don't want her left alone for very long," Ryan told Lil once she'd pointed out the spot in the woods.

"You think whoever tried to run her down will try something else?" The glint of anger in the woman's eyes proved what he'd already known about her. She was like a mama bear when it came to Shandra.

"They could." He watched as the woman hobbled from footprint to footprint, leaning on the walking stick as she hurried back to the house.

He stared into the trees and decided to go in the barn and get a pair of snowshoes. It would make navigating the snow much easier.

He walked to the front of the barn and opened the big door. Light filled the barn, glinting off Shandra's Jeep. The driver's door was open on the vehicle. She'd never walk off and leave the door open. And Lil would have closed it when she did chores.

Ryan pulled his revolver from the back of his waistband and ducked in behind the door where the sun didn't shine. He walked along the wall in the murky darkness, peering around the interior of the barn.

His leg bumped into something seconds before he felt his body toppling forward. Before he could stabilize, someone hit him from behind, knocking him to the floor. Ryan twisted to confront his attacker and something struck his head. He heard two voices as he struggled to remain conscience. "Get a rope. We'll tie him up. I'm not killing a cop."

The female voice was familiar, domineering. He sank into darkness as his arms were pulled behind his back.

***

Shandra woke to arguing.

"Get out of here!" Lil's rough voice demanded.

"Woof!" Sheba trotted to the back door.

Shandra didn't have time to think before Tabby and a man with shoulder-length, black hair and a tattoo on his neck entered the room. The man had a hold of Lil's arm. Tabby had a revolver that looked like Ryan's.

"Ryan? Where's Ryan?" Shandra's dream was coming true.

"He's in the barn," Tabby said.

"Did you kill him like you did Carl and Alexis?" Shandra knew this was bold talk. They didn't have any proof, but if Tabby did kill Ryan, she was going to make sure the woman got everything coming to her.

Ned's gaze started darting between Tabby and Shandra. "What does she mean Alexis?"

"She's just trying to get us upset." Tabby glared at her. "Where's the keys to your Jeep? He couldn't figure out how to hotwire it."

Shandra stared at the woman. If she could stall long enough, Pete and the searchers would arrive. "Why would I tell you?"

Tabby sneered. "To keep a bullet out of that big ugly mutt." She pointed the revolver at Sheba who cowered at Shandra's feet.

Shandra pointed to the bedroom door. "Sheba, go!" The dog leaped to her feet and bounded into the bedroom, she even closed the door. "Find the keys yourself."

The woman glared at her. "Ned, go search for the keys."

"Where?" he asked.

"The whole house. Think, where do you keep your keys? Look!" Tabby grabbed Lil's arm and pulled her away from Ned, shoving her toward the couch.

Shandra caught Lil, landing her softer on the couch than Tabby had intended.

Drawers opened and closed in the kitchen. Shandra thought back to the last time she'd driven the Jeep. It was the day Carl died. Since then Ryan had been driving her everywhere. The keys were in the coat pocket of her ski jacket, which was in Ryan's truck. As long as they didn't decide to take his truck, they'd never find the keys.

She smiled, leaned back, and raced through all the

information they knew. "Is Dana Benham part of this?"

Tabby took a chair but kept the revolver pointed at them. "Dana is my aunt."

"Does she know you kill people?"

"You don't know if I killed anyone." Tabby glanced toward the back door as the dryer buzzer pealed down the hall.

"You're holding a gun on us and look pretty comfortable doing it. You were the only person, besides Ned who slipped that note to Carl, to know about the meeting on the mountain. I think Ned wanted to confront his father, and you followed to kill Carl." Shandra spotted Ned standing in the hall listening.

"Carl was the devil. What he did to all those women, you included. I'm surprised someone didn't kill him sooner." Tabby slipped out of her coat. It was the same color as the coat Alexis had worn to the diner. "You keep it nice and toasty in here."

"It was pretty heartless the way you blackmailed his past victims." Shandra wasn't going to let this woman off the hook for anything.

Tabby huffed. "One of them or their spouse was supposed to get mad enough they'd kill Carl. That was the plan. I couldn't even get Shelly's brother riled up enough to kill him." She stood up and paced toward the fireplace. "What is wrong with people when they don't stand up for the people they say they love?"

Shandra latched onto this tidbit. "Who didn't stand up for you? Your father?"

"That's none of your business! I'm helping the only person who cares." Tabby paced back to the chair and pointed the weapon at them. "You were the one they were supposed to think killed Carl. We planted clues. How were we supposed to know you were dating a cop?"

Ned walked into the room. "I can't find the keys. Let's just take the truck they came in."

"We can't. That belongs to a cop. We don't need that kind of grief." Tabby sat down. Her bottom lip disappeared between her teeth as she stared at Lil and Shandra.

Chapter Thirty-two

Ryan woke and struggled with the rope securing his hands. He moved his feet and was surprised to see they weren't tied. Pushing to his feet, he scanned the barn. The two who'd knocked him out had left the door open.

He went to the area where Lil kept the tack and backed up to the shelf holding the brushes, hoof picks, and hoof knives. He put his back to the shelf and fingered the handles until he felt the square wooden handle of a hoof knife. Twisting his hand, he cut at the rope with the blade. It wasn't as sharp as a real knife but it would have to do. His knife was attached to his belt out of reach of his tied hands.

Ryan's mind raced in twenty different directions. Who jumped him? Ms. Vincent and Ned or someone else? He knew what he'd caught them trying to do, hotwire the Jeep. With him tied up out here they could ransack the house and possibly hurt Shandra while looking for the keys. He hoped Shandra gave them the keys and got them out of here. The state police could put a bolo out on her Jeep and apprehend them.

The rope gave way. He dropped the hoof knife on the floor and headed out the back door of the barn. Sneaking along the back of the studio, he heard the squeak and crunch of tires approaching.

Ryan ran to the front of the building and spotted Pete's SUV and two cars behind him coming up the drive. He punched Pete's number and prayed they didn't hit the open meadow before Pete answered.

"Ryan we're—"

"Stop! Don't drive any farther," Ryan ordered.

The front SUV stopped.

"What's going on?"

"I'm not sure. Two people jumped me in the barn and tied me up. I think they're in the house with Shandra and Lil. I was just headed to see when I spotted you coming. Give me a minute to see who we're dealing with." Ryan glanced at the back door. So far no one had looked out that he could tell.

"I'll get the others ready to back you up."

Ryan shoved the phone in his pocket and ran to the back of the house. He'd use the patio doors to do reconnaissance.

***

Shandra caught a glimpse of someone peeking in the patio door. She immediately diverted her attention.

"There was a beater truck in the lean-to off the barn. Does that work?" Tabby asked.

Shandra glanced at Ned. Why did he let her call the shots?

"You take my truck and that's the last time you'll touch anyone's wheels," Lil said, glaring at Tabby.

"So it runs?" Tabby pointed the revolver at Lil. "Where's the keys? I bet they're in it. Ned go take a look. While you're out there, make sure that cop is still tied up."

Shandra's tension eased. They hadn't killed Ryan. The color of the hair she'd seen in the window, she had a pretty good idea it was Ryan. Knowing he was out there, made her bolder. Braver.

"Where is Alexis? She left her room last night at eleven. Your usual tryst time, but she never returned to her room. Did she become a casualty?" Shandra leaned forward and poured herself more tea.

Lil's leg bumped hers.

She glanced over and smiled. Lil stared at her like she was crazy.

"I met Alexis last night. That woman was as meek as her brother was demanding. Poor Elizabeth, going through life cleaning up after her son and loathing a daughter who was weak."

"What do you mean cleaning up after her son?" Shandra was intrigued to hear about the Landers' dirty laundry.

"After you got away from Carl, Elizabeth hired my aunt to keep tabs on him and help others get away. Elizabeth hoped that he'd give up ruining the lives of co-eds and go play with prostitutes. But he didn't. He liked the game of luring in the unsuspecting young women and then dominating them. None of them knew he videoed their times in bed." She smiled. "He didn't start that until after you. Though he mentioned several times after seeing you at the art show he wished he'd thought of it sooner."

Shandra shuddered. How had I been so foolish to

fall for his falseness?

"Did Elizabeth suggest you blackmail the women in hopes they'd kill her son?" Even as she said it, Shandra couldn't believe a woman would think so little of her son she'd plot his murder.

"Yes. Of course, my aunt didn't know I was helping Elizabeth. She thought I was friends with Alexis." Tabby glanced to the back door.

"It's taking Ned a long time to check on the pickup," Shandra said, hoping Tabby would wander to the back door.

"Yes, it is. Makes me wonder if your cop got loose." Tabby stood and strode over to the couch. "Come on." She grabbed Shandra's arm and yanked her to her feet.

The woman was strong.

She pointed the revolver at Lil. "Get in that room with the dog."

Lil shook her head, a stubborn set to her jaw.

"Go in with Sheba," Shandra said, winking at Lil.

"I don't like you going anywhere with that lunatic," Lil said, making one last stand.

"Go. I'll be fine. Tabby doesn't have a reason to kill me." Shandra hoped her words were true.

"Then why'd she try to run you down?" Lil stood.

Tabby pulled Shandra away from the couch. "Because she's sticking her nose where it don't belong."

"That's because you dragged me into the murder by making me look like a suspect." She twisted and faced Tabby. "Whose idea was it to make me look guilty?"

Tabby sneered. "Mine! After seeing you in

Albuquerque, you were all Carl talked about. I figured the way he had such an infatuation with you it would be easy to talk him into coming here to see you. But his gaze started roving the minute we arrived and I couldn't let him ruin another woman. I'd promised Elizabeth when I moved in with Carl, I'd keep him from hurting anymore young women. He had to die before he did."

Shandra stared into Tabby's eyes. The woman thought of herself as a crusader. "Where did Ned come in? Why did he try to run me down?"

"I told him you knew too much. That we'd have to think of some way to keep you from digging more. He made that stupid attempt to hit you with the car." Tabby glanced at Lil. "Go get in that room."

"Go." Shandra said.

Lil headed to the room, slowly. She peered out until the door clicked shut.

Tabby shoved Shandra toward the kitchen and the window. They both peered out. There wasn't any movement near the lean-to where Lil's pickup sat.

"I don't like this," Tabby muttered.

"Put your hands up!"

Shandra had never been so happy to hear Ryan's voice.

Tabby shoved the revolver into Shandra's side. "She's dead if you don't tell me where Ned is."

Ryan dropped his hands to his side. The revolver he'd pointed at Tabby hung in his hand. "He's outside with the state police. This house is surrounded and you haven't a chance."

"I don't believe you!" Tabby snapped.

"Believe him." Pete stepped into the kitchen from the back door, his revolver aimed at Tabby's head.

"And if you don't believe me, look out the window."

Tabby turned to the window. An officer in a vest that said SWAT had a rifle aimed at the window.

Ryan used the distraction to move around the counter. He lunged, pulling Tabby's arm that held the gun, away from Shandra as Pete pulled Shandra away from Tabby.

A shot rang out.

The bullet sunk into the cupboard.

Tabby struggled, kicking, biting, and cursing. Another officer rushed in, cuffing her and leading her out of the house.

No sooner had Tabby left his hands, than they were wrapped around Shandra. "Are you okay," he asked.

"I'm fine. Did you get Ned?" She snuggled her head against his chest.

Lil ran into the kitchen a rifle in her hands, her eyes wide. "I heard a shot."

Shandra raised her head. "Everything's fine. The police have her."

"I'll be back to take your statements as soon as I give instructions."

Ryan nodded to Pete and continued to hold Shandra. If they kept getting drawn into murder investigations, he wasn't sure his heart could take it.

Chapter Thirty-three

Ryan drove up Shandra's drive. He'd been back to work for a week and was ready to spend time with her. After giving their statements, he'd spent the night pampering Shandra. While she still wasn't ready to take the step of sharing her bed, they'd kissed and embraced for several hours before they went to their separate bedrooms.

Sheba bounded out the studio door as it opened at his approach. Shandra stood in the doorway.

He climbed out of his truck and walked to the studio. "Hello." He kissed her like he'd wanted to do from the first day they met.

She returned the kiss, clasped his hand and led him into the studio. "I finished it."

Sitting on a table was a stunning vase. The colors were bursts of pinks, yellows, and green. The cheerfulness of the colors reminded him of a spring meadow in bloom. He walked closer, taking in the carved images in the vase. They were of a girl with chains on her feet and hands. She grew and the chains on her feet were gone. Again she reflected more maturity and the chains on her hands were broken and she smiled.

"It's beautiful!" Ryan pulled Shandra into an embrace.

"I'm donating it to the women's center in Albuquerque. I told Dana they can either keep it to show women they are strong or auction it off to help fund the facility."

They had both been happy to hear Dana knew nothing about her niece's plan to get her hooks into the Landers' money. The woman had been suspicious of her niece's actions, but Tabitha always came up with plausible reasons for her actions.

"How do you feel?" Ryan peered into her eyes. He saw the strong, confident woman he'd witnessed that first day. Her eyes weren't shadowed or wary. She'd shed the layer of her past that had kept her isolated.

"Like I'm starting a new life."

Shandra smiled at Ryan and led him out of the studio. In the kitchen, she poured wine and led him into the main room. They both sat on the couch.

"Have you learned any more about Alexis?" When Pete had finished taking their statements over a week ago, no one knew where Alexis Landers had gone.

"Her body was discovered in the laundry chute at the lodge."

Shandra shivered. "I had a feeling she wasn't alive. Especially when I saw Tabby wearing Alexis' coat."

"Ms. Vincent killed Alexis in the exercise room. She'd met Alexis at her room and kept the door open enough she could go back later and exchange her coat for Alexis'. She wanted people to see Alexis leaving the lodge but the desk clerk had seen Ms. Vincent enough she knew it was her. The whole coat switching didn't work."

Shandra shook her head. "I don't understand. Why kill either of them?"

"Mrs. Landers saw the good things her grandson was doing and decided she would make him her only heir. The problem with that was her late husband left his estate to her and his children. Which meant when she died all the money would go to Carl and Alexis and nothing would go to Ned because Carl had given up his rights to the boy and didn't want anything to do with him."

"Why didn't she just start giving him money? It would be better than killing people." Shandra would never understand how some people thought.

"She also knew with her gone she couldn't keep cleaning up Carl's messes. She wanted him gone, according to Ms. Vincent. Mrs. Landers and Ned have lawyered up and aren't saying a word." Ryan sipped his wine.

"Did Elizabeth really want Alexis killed? She was malleable as far as I could see. She could have talked Alexis into giving money to Ned." Shandra put her hand on Sheba's head as it settled on her lap.

"That was all Ms. Vincent. It seems she decided Alexis had to go for Ned to get it all. And she planned to marry Ned." Ryan captured her hand. "I'm glad you are finally free of the past. But I want you to know, you could have told me about Landers and how he treated you. I wouldn't have thought any less of you."

"I know that now. The hurt, physical and mental,

isn't something I want to ever experience again. I have finally found who I am and who I want to be."

Shandra smiled. "I see who you are. You are exactly what I see, no hidden personalities or fetishes. I won't keep secrets from you and I know you won't keep secrets from me."

About the Author

Award-winning author Paty Jager and her husband raise alfalfa hay in rural eastern Oregon. On her road to publication she wrote freelance articles for two local newspapers and enjoyed her job with the County Extension service as a 4-H Program Assistant. Raising hay and cattle, riding horses, and battling rattlesnakes, she not only writes the western lifestyle, she lives it.

http://www.patyjager.net

To learn how to get FREE and discounted books sign up for Paty's free newsletter.

http://eepurl.com/1CFgX

To join Paty's Facebook Fan page here:

https://www.facebook.com/PatyJagerAuthor/

Shandra Higheagle Mystery Series

Double Duplicity

Tarnished Remains

Deadly Aim

Murderous Secrets

Killer Descent

Windtree
Press

Thank you for purchasing this Windtree Press publication. For other books of the heart, please visit our website at www.windtreepress.com.

For questions or more information contact us

at info@windtreepress.com.

Windtree Press

www.windtreepress.com

Hillsboro, OR

Made in the USA
Charleston, SC
02 April 2016